RIGHT

Jana Aston

Edited by RJ Locksley
Cover Design by JA Huss
Cover Model Robert Reider
Photographer Omar Sorbellini
Formatting: Erik Gevers

Dedication

To every single one of you that read WRONG, thank you.
I wrote it thinking no one would read it, but you did.
I hope I don't let you down with RIGHT.

One

I slide into the passenger seat of the low-slung car as the door thuds shut behind me and busy myself with the seatbelt, using the opportunity to watch him as he crosses the front of the car. His strides are confident, unhurried. The fingers of his left hand skim the hood before he rounds the headlight and reaches the driver's side door.

I suddenly feel uneasy, and I never feel uneasy.

This car is too small for the both of us. I'm annoyed at the idea of being cooped up inside the same ten square feet as him all the way to Philadelphia. I just met him twenty minutes ago. Why is he having this effect on me?

The door handle clicks and he's behind the wheel, the engine purring a second later. I watch him buckle himself in from the corner of my eye, but keep my head straight, my focus on my hands folded in my lap, until the silence goes on too long. He's staring at me, the car idling, apparently content to wait until he has my attention. I turn my head and meet his eyes. They're brown, another check mark completing tall, dark and handsome. They light up with amusement as he speaks, which unsettles me. Why?

"How can you possibly think Finn Camden is the right man for you?"

That's why.

Two

Sixteen Years Ago

I clutch my brand-new Strawberry Shortcake backpack in my lap and check the window again. We're getting close, and it's my job to make sure I get off the bus at the right stop. I'm in first grade this year, not a kindergartener baby, and I get to take the bus home from school. My brother Eric is meeting me at the bus stop. He's a teenager and that's his job. To pick me up. I know he won't forget, because he loves me. Also, 'cause Mom said he'd be grounded for a week if he forgot.

The bus turns onto Norrans Drive. This is my stop. I grip my backpack tighter and eye the distance to the door.

"Everly!" Timmy Stuart pops his head over the seat in front of me. He's missing a tooth and his hair is a disaster. It's a disaster because he let me cut it. Mom says I need a lot of supervision. I don't think his hair would have turned out any better if she'd been watching me though, so I don't think that's true.

"I saved one of my new pencils for you," he says, holding it up.

I grin back at him. The kid has had a crush on me since Pre-K. I should really stop messing with his hair. "Thanks, Timmy," I tell him, and slip the pencil into a side pocket on my bag. "You want one of my erasers?" I offer, holding up a pink strawberry-shaped eraser, which he takes.

The bus stops and I rush to the front. I see Eric waiting as

3

the doors swoosh open. I slide my backpack straps over my shoulders and hop down the bus steps onto the sidewalk. I bet I can get Eric to let me have some of the candy he's got stashed in his room instead of the yogurt I'm supposed to have for my after-school snack.

But a second later I stop short, candy forgotten. There's a boy with Eric. I've never seen him before. He must be a new high-school friend—it's Eric's first year of high school. His friend is cute. Really cute.

"This your little sister, Eric?" The boy smiles at me.

"Yup, this is Bever—"

"Everly," I interrupt. "My name is Everly."

"Not according to Mom and Dad it isn't."

I stop gazing at the boy long enough to glare at Eric. The boy laughs. "Why don't I just call you Shortcake?" he asks, and he extends his hand like I'm an adult, not a kid. "My name is Finn."

I shake his hand and it's settled, in my six-year-old heart. I'm going to marry Finn.

Then he leans over and ruffles my hair.

Humph. Looks like I've got my work cut out for me.

Three

Present Day

I break his gaze and turn back to the windshield, crossing my legs and tossing my hair over my right shoulder. His eyes annoy me. They're too inquisitive. I've never been this fascinating to anyone, ever. And I'm not interested in being the object of this man's fascination. "Finn and I are perfect together," I snap. "Just take me home," I say, waving dismissively at the stationary car.

"Finn and you aren't together," he replies and pulls the car onto Ridgebury heading towards Salem.

I shrug and slip my phone out of my pocket and tap the screen to life.

"What are you doing?"

What does it look like I'm doing? "Checking my messages," I reply. "Can we be done talking now?"

He makes a noise that sounds a bit like a grunt and then pushes a button on the steering wheel before saying, "Call Sandra."

Huh. He's gonna grunt at me for checking messages and then call his girlfriend on speakerphone? Whatever. The ringing ends as a woman answers, "Yes, sir?"

Yes, sir? I pause mid-tap and dart my eyes across the center divide. Yup. Sex freak. Bet he makes her ask permission to come. Hell to the no. I shake my head and return my attention where it belongs, on my phone. I can't believe he's going to make me listen while he orders his submissive to strip and wait for him next to the front door. He's probably gonna make her kneel too. What an asshole.

"Sandra, I need one of the IT guys to send me the feeds for all of Everly Jensen's social media accounts."

Wait. What?

"She's a senior at Penn. Grew up in Ridgefield, Connecticut. You should be able to locate her easily enough."

"What are you doing?" I interrupt, confused and annoyed.

"Facebook, Twitter, Instagram," he rattles off. "And whatever other sites college girls are currently using to post selfies on the internet. That will be all, Sandra." He ends the call with a tap to a control on the steering wheel.

"Hello, I'm sitting right here. Did you want me to friend-request you or something?" I wave the phone in my hand as I talk. "Because that"—I point in the direction of the speakers in the dashboard—"was a little melodramatic."

"You were more interested in your phone than talking. So I'm curious about what's online that you find so fascinating."

We're on Titcus Road, headed towards I-684, traffic is light, people still enjoying the long Thanksgiving holiday weekend. And I'm still annoyed. This is not the drive back to school I had planned.

"That's called stalking, not curiosity," I say, my interest in what my friends are up to forgotten.

He laughs. The fucker actually laughs at me. "So it's okay for you to stalk Finn, but it's not okay for me to stalk you? You're priceless, Everly. I think I'm really going to enjoy you."

"Enjoy me? You don't have me."

"I will."

Four

Ten Years Ago

"Chloe, he's here," I whisper.

"One second," she replies before I hear her yelling to her mom, "I'm going to Everly's!" There's a muffled reply from her mom and then she confirms she's on her way.

"Attic," I whisper again.

"Gotcha." And the line goes dead.

Four minutes later the screen door slams as Chloe arrives. The stairs creak as she jogs up and then she appears in view as she walks through our second-floor game room.

"She's in her room," Eric calls out to Chloe as she walks past and heads towards my closed door down the hall.

"I know, thanks!"

She disappears out of sight but my door cracks open and then closed as she makes her way into my room. A second later she's boosting herself through the open attic entrance inside my walk-in closet via the dresser I've placed below it for this very reason.

"Hey," she whispers as she tiptoes across the floor joists until she reaches the platform I've set up next to the vent leading into the game room. She lies down on the sleeping bag I've laid out. "What are they doing?"

"Playing video games." We're whispering, but luckily the games they like to play are pretty loud, so we don't have to be very quiet. "He looks good in that Eagles jersey, doesn't he?"

7

Chloe nods. "So cute."

"I love baseball."

"The Eagles play football, Everly."

"Oh." I pause. "Well, I've got plenty of time to learn about football. I'm only twelve. He's not going to take me seriously until I'm at least sixteen."

"Probably not," Chloe agrees.

I flip open my notebook. It's pink and says *Dreams & Schemes* on the front cover in gold cursive. It's where I keep all of my Finn Camden notes. I draw pictures in it too. I'm getting pretty good. I add a note to remind myself to learn about the Eagles before flipping to the back. That's where I practice writing Everly Camden. Mrs. Camden. Mrs. Finn Camden. I'm already really good at it, but practicing never hurt anybody.

We're quiet then, watching Finn and Eric through the vent until Chloe speaks.

"My dad cancelled."

"What? Why?" She was supposed to go to New York next week to visit him. Her parents divorced three years ago and she hardly ever sees her dad anymore.

"He said he had a business trip." She shrugs, but I see the tears welling up in her eyes.

He's so stupid.

"Well, he's dumb and I have an even better idea," I say, throwing an arm around her.

"What?" She wipes her eyes and composes herself. She doesn't allow herself to get upset very often.

"I bet you can come with us to Hershey Park! I'm gonna ask my parents tonight. I know they'll say yes." They will too. Because my parents are the best. "We'll go on all the rollercoasters. And then we'll go on the fun slide even though we're too old. And we'll spend an entire day at the water park. Plus, I have forty dollars saved up and we will buy all the candy, Chloe. All of it."

"Maybe," she says, but she smiles. "What are you going to do this fall when Eric and Finn leave for college?" Chloe asks, done talking about her dad.

I sigh sadly. "Well, I've got my notebook," I say, tapping it with my pen. "So I can study." I stop speaking as the game silences in the room below us. Chloe and I crowd over the vent to watch as Eric and Finn toss the remotes on the ottoman and take off down the stairs. "Wait," I say, holding up a finger. We listen until the fridge slams shut. "They're getting a snack, let's go."

I drop through the attic entrance into my closet and immediately head to my vanity table to check my appearance. I'm not allowed to have makeup yet, so applying Bonne Bell lip smacker in strawberry and combing my hair will have to do.

Chloe and I stroll into the kitchen a minute later to find the guys loading pizza rolls into the oven.

"Oh, I didn't know you guys were using the oven. We were gonna make cookies," I announce. I even manage to look surprised to see them in the kitchen. Hey, I'm twelve, not six.

"No worries, Shortcake. We'll be done with the oven in ten minutes." Finn grins at me and I lose my focus for a second. He needs a haircut. His sandy brown hair is floppier than normal.

"What kind of cookies do you guys like?" I ask, directing the question at Finn as I head to the pantry. "We'll bring some up to you when they're done." I add a smile but Finn is peering into the oven at the pizza rolls and misses it.

"You know I like chocolate chip," Eric responds and I panic. I want to know what Finn likes.

"Uh, yeah, but your friend is over," I say, waving at Finn. "It's polite to ask what your guests want." I smile. There. That was smooth, right?

Eric looks at me like I've lost my mind, but I ignore him and focus on Finn. "Finn, what kind of cookies do you like?"

"Huh?" He pauses from chugging a Coke to look at me. "Um, chocolate-chip cookies are fine with me."

"Yep, who doesn't love chocolate-chip cookies and football, right?" Wait. Did that even make sense? I sound like an idiot. Flirting is hard.

"Football?" Finn questions.

"Your jersey," I say, nodding towards him as I set the ingredients on the counter. Chloe is already there with the mixing bowl and wooden spoon. "Go Eagles!" I say and do a little fist bump and immediately want to die. That was so stupid.

"Oh." Finn glances down at his jersey. "My brother gave this to me."

"I love football!" I gush and Eric stops and looks at me strangely. Okay. Too far.

"I'm so glad you've learned to like football, Everly," Eric says slowly.

Oh, no. He's gonna call me out on this. I went too far. I should never have read those teen dating columns on the internet. I am clearly not ready for teenage-level flirting. I duck my head and pray.

"Dad is going to be so happy."

What? I peek a look at Eric. He's rubbing his chin and waiting for me to pay attention.

"Dad's gonna be so happy he has someone to watch football with every weekend," he says with a smirk.

Crud.

Five

Present Day

"Why does he call you Shortcake, anyway?" he asks, glancing at me. His left arm is casually bent against the door frame, fingers resting on the steering wheel. His right hand rests on his thigh. He fills out the pants he's wearing nicely. I can see the outline of muscle on his leg. My gaze lingers, wondering if I can see the outline of something else as well.

No! I mentally chastise myself. *He's not the one I'm interested in.*

"I always assumed you were a freckle-faced little redhead," he continues, "or that you possibly looked like a Cabbage Patch doll."

"Hey!"

His lips twist in amusement at my ire. We're stopped dead in traffic on the I-684. He slides an arm over my headrest and turns his full attention in my direction. He leans towards me, his head inches from mine, and while he's not touching me, it feels like he's all over me. It feels... intimate. "But you're beautiful."

Oh.

Oh, no.

His eyes run across my face and I wonder what he sees there. Denial? Sheer panic? Attraction? I swallow and it sounds loud in this small space. He smells good. Why does he have to smell good? I'm so annoyed. He's got a hint of stubble across his jaw and I find myself wondering what that would feel like pressed against my neck. Stop thinking. I need to stop thinking. Or start thinking about something else. Like orphaned kangaroos.

He takes my silence as license to continue speaking. "Stunning, actually. Your hair, Jesus." Traffic picks up and he settles back into his seat as the car moves forward. "It's not red."

"No."

"I can't wait to run my hands through it," he says and I suck in a breath. "Or wrap it around my fist to pull you closer, or yank your head back while I've got you bent over—"

"Stop it!" It comes out a little breathless, even to my own ears.

He laughs, but continues in a less sexual tone. "It's... the color of a goddamned melted Hershey bar is what it is. I can't imagine you were a redheaded child, so Shortcake doesn't make sense, and Finn's a pretty logical guy."

"I was carrying a Strawberry Shortcake backpack when we met," I finally mumble.

"Excuse me?" He looks genuinely thrown for a minute, glancing at me as the car moves through traffic.

"I was carrying a Strawberry Shortcake backpack when we met."

He moves the hand from his thigh to his mouth. I'm not sure why, because he's laughing too hard to cover it up.

"I was six, asshole!"

He calms himself and nods. "I need a pet name for you then, if I'm going to compete with Finn for your affections."

"There's no competition."

"You're right. Finn isn't competing, so the game's mine." He shoots me a wink and I groan. "Commando."

"What?"

"I'll call you Commando," he replies. "Since we're doing nicknames based on first meetings."

It takes me a second to process what he's saying. "I'm wearing underwear!"

He nods. "Good. Tell me about them."

"No! You're really aggressive, you know that?"

"Coming from you I'll take that as a compliment."

"Yeah, okay," I say dismissively and cross my legs. I tap on my phone screen wondering if I can calculate how much longer I'm going to be trapped in this car.

"Boots."

"What?" I wonder if there's something wrong with him. Isn't there a disorder that causes people to randomly blurt out words that make no sense? That's probably what he has. I'm gonna check on WebMD.

"I'll call you Boots," he says, nodding at my legs. I'm wearing brown knee-high boots, my jeans tucked into them. My legs look incredible. I planned this outfit from head to toe. For Finn. "Since you vetoed Commando, we'll go with Boots."

I blow out a breath. "Fine."

Six

"Chloe, zip me up, please." I turn my back to her, holding the front of my homecoming dress against my chest to hold the dress up.

"Done," she announces and I move to the mirror to check my reflection. Jewelry's on. Hair's done. Killer high heels I've had to negotiate for since school started are on my feet. I turn my attention to Chloe. She looks perfect, but she's tugging at her dress in a way that belies her discomfort.

"Stop fidgeting. You're beautiful. Own it."

She drops her hands and stands a little straighter, then darts a look in the mirror to verify what I'm saying. Chloe would happily do nothing but study and pad her college resume with volunteer projects if it weren't for me forcing her to experience high school. She is beautiful, when she's not hiding behind an oversized sweatshirt and a stack of textbooks. Her hair is almost red, but not quite—too much brown intermixed to make her truly a redhead—but she's got a sprinkling of freckles, true to her Irish heritage.

"Let's go downstairs and wait for Tim and Dave. They should be here any second and Mom will want a million pictures." I check my clutch to make sure my lipstick is still there. Then I check Chloe's for her because she'd never think to put it there in the first place.

We're on the bottom step when I hear him. Finn Camden

is here. My heart pounds and I pause abruptly in the foyer, causing Chloe to bump into me. I haven't seen Finn in two years. Not since the summer after he graduated from college. I couldn't have planned this better if I'd tried, and believe me, I've tried. There's no way he can't notice me looking like this. *Notice* me. Like I'm a woman, not a little kid. Not Eric's little sister.

"Who the hell allowed you to get those shoes?" Eric emerges from the basement stairwell carrying one of the chairs to an old dining set that's been taking up space in the basement ever since Mom replaced ours a few years ago.

Finn appears a moment later with a matching chair. His hair is tousled and he's got the hint of a summer tan left. He's wearing athletic shorts and a gray t-shirt and I try to ogle as much as I can with my brother standing right next to him. I take a mental picture so I can write down every detail of this encounter in my diary later.

"Shortcake!" He smiles at me and I wait for it. For that flash of recognition to cross his face. The one that says I'm not a child anymore. The one that says he finds me attractive. The one I've been waiting for my entire life. But I get... nothing. Just the same friendly grin I've gotten my whole life.

"Dad, are you letting her leave the house in those shoes?"

Dad has just emerged from the basement with a third chair and Eric doesn't waste a second letting his opinion on my footwear be known. Thank God he never moved back in after college. I'd have died a virgin. He's more protective than both of our parents combined.

"That's between your mother and Everly. I stay out of it," Dad tells him as he kisses my forehead. "You look lovely, princess," he says to me. "Be good and don't wear yourself out tonight. You don't want to fall asleep again during the football game tomorrow."

Ugh. I see Eric smirking at me from the corner of my eye but I ignore him.

"What are you guys doing?" I nod to the chairs.

"Mom's donating our old table set to Finn's new

apartment." Eric slaps Finn on the back. "He got a job at Penn. This fool is going to be teaching the future of America."

"I don't know about the future of America, buddy. A few thousand Economics students, maybe." Finn shrugs and it's the cutest thing I've ever seen. He's grown up, I realize. He's filled out. Not the skinny high school boy I remember. He's fit, with a runner's physique, and I remember that he ran cross-country for Summit High School.

I joined cross-country freshman year. It was the worst afternoon of my high-school life. So we aren't going to be one of those couples who jog together. No biggie.

They head out the door with the dining chairs as I turn to Chloe. "Well, looks like we're going to Penn. College decision done."

"Well, one of us has the transcript for Penn," she says slowly, wrinkling her nose at me.

"Ugh. How hard could it be?" I eye the door, hoping for another glimpse of Finn.

Chloe pinches the bridge of her nose. "It's Ivy League, Everly."

"So I'll *Legally Blonde* myself together."

"Good plan. You remember how that movie ended, don't you?"

I nod. "She gets the guy."

"Not the guy she got into law school for."

Humph. Sometimes Chloe is just so literal. "It's an outline, Chloe. We can edit as we go."

There's a commotion at the door as Tim and Dave arrive, followed by Dad, Eric and Finn. I check Finn's face for jealousy. Nope. None. Tim's eyes bug out when he sees me though, which mollifies me slightly. Eric slaps a firm hand on his shoulder and leans in, I assume to threaten him. Meanwhile, Dave shuffles over to Chloe with an awkward hello. She is never getting laid.

"Pictures!" Mom emerges from the kitchen with her professional-grade camera. She's a middle-school librarian, not a photographer. I'm not sure which she loves more—slicing open a new case of books for the library shelves, or documenting her children's milestones on film.

She named us after the authors of her favorite children's books. She even decorated both of our nurseries in honor of our namesakes. I know this because there are pictures.

It's junior year. I know the drill by now. The sooner we take the obligatory shots, the sooner we can leave for the dance. I grab Tim's hand and lead him to the fireplace. Mom loves this shot. Behind her Eric is doing the universal, "I'm watching you," gesture, pointing two fingers from his eyes to Tim's. "Ignore him," I tell Tim. "Smile for my mom so we can get out of here."

I glance over at Finn, but he's not looking in my direction at all. He's glancing at his phone and saying goodbye to Eric. He's not even interested enough to look? I know I'm still young, but he could *look*. He's just too good a guy, I decide. He still views me as Eric's little sister. Off limits. But that will change when I turn eighteen. I know it will. I'll get into Penn. He'll see me as an adult—a young one, but legal. And eventually he'll see me as so much more.

I can be patient.

Seven

Present

"You're not saving yourself for him, are you?"

I'm checking my Facebook when he starts talking again. I stop on a picture in my timeline. My friend Sophie just posted pictures from Thanksgiving with her new boyfriend. Those two are looking awfully cozy. Let's see what else she posted this weekend. I click on her profile but I don't get to see much because a second later the phone is removed from my grasp and slid into the inside breast pocket of his blazer.

"That's my phone."

"This is my car."

"So?"

"So we're getting to know one another and you're being rude."

Is this guy nuts? I eye his pocket and decide it's a lost cause while he's driving. Sighing, I fold my hands in my lap and watch the traffic. "We're not getting to know each other. You're giving me a lift home, and that's the end of this story." I lift a finger to gesture between us.

"Back to my question. Are you saving yourself for Finn?" He tilts his head in my direction and cocks an eyebrow in question.

Is he seriously asking me if I'm still a virgin?

"I'm twenty-two, asshole. I'm practicing for Finn, not saving myself for him."

There's a hint of a smirk on his face that makes me want to punch him, or watch porn with him. I'm not sure which and it confuses me. I wish he wasn't so attractive. He'd be easier to ignore.

He runs a hand over his jaw. I think he's trying to wipe the smirk off of his annoying face. "Glad to hear it, Everly, glad to hear it."

"Are you?" I don't care what his thoughts are on my sex life. My question is sarcasm, at best. "I think it's weird that you have an opinion about my sexual history and rude that you're bringing it up." There.

He nods. "I'm glad you'll appreciate what you're getting."

"What?"

"I'm glad you'll appreciate me."

I lean against the window and stare at him.

"I've been practicing as well," he continues.

"For a lot longer," I interrupt.

He grins. "Right. I've been practicing longer than you have and I'm glad to know you have a baseline to judge me by."

"A baseline." I turn a bit in my seat so I can tuck my left leg onto the seat. "A baseline is what we're calling my sexual experience?"

He shrugs. "Yeah. Unless you wanna tell me their names. We'll go with baseline. Did you want to get into specifics?" He runs his gaze over my face while I pull my right leg up onto the seat and really get comfortable.

"Because you're better?"

"Yes."

"Cocky."

"Confident."

I put up a hand. "So you're glad I'm having sex with other men. Because you think I'm going to sleep with you at some point and I'll be blown away by your mad sexual skills?"

"Had."

I lift an eyebrow in question.

"I'm glad you've *had* sex with other men. In the past." He checks the rearview and changes lanes. I watch his profile while he maneuvers the car. He is confident, I'll give him that. From the moment I met him, an hour ago, he's not shown me a moment of anything other than exhausting confidence. "You are a bit younger than me."

"A lot."

He glowers at me. "I'm four years older than Finn. It's hardly any different."

I shrug.

"So you're younger than I am. I'm glad you won't have to wonder if it's different between us. Because you'll know that it is. The second I lay a finger on you, you'll know."

See what I mean about the confidence?

Eight

Three Years Ago

I survey the disaster that is my new room in Stroh Hall at the University of Pennsylvania. Half my clothes are lying on the unmade bed. My desk is covered with toiletries. Bags of stuff cover the floor. But the mini-fridge is plugged in. That's a start.

"Are you sure you don't want us to stay and help you unpack?" My mom eyes the mess with a worried frown. "I could find your sheets and make the bed at least."

"Helen, come on. Let's hit the road. Everly is going to combust if we don't get out of her hair." My dad puts an arm around her shoulders and kisses her forehead. "She's only going to be three hours away, honey."

My mom plants a smile on her face and hugs me. "We're so proud of you, Everly."

"I know, Mom."

Dad winks at me from the door. She's having a hard time with the idea of being an empty-nester. My dad's taking it just fine and has planned a surprise trip to Paris to celebrate and help distract her. They're leaving tomorrow evening. He's going to pick up fresh croissants for breakfast and tell her to pack her bags. My parents are adorable. Perfect, really.

They had my brother just a couple of years out of college, and me eight years after that, so they're still young. Well, young for parents of grown children. They both celebrated their fiftieth birthdays during my senior year, and they're healthy, active people. I get my dark hair from my mom. Hers is shorter than mine, but still the same chocolate color. Dad's turning a little grey, but his hair is much lighter than ours to begin with. It looks good on him, distinguished. They could easily pass for parents of middle-schoolers, instead of an eighteen- and a twenty-six-year-old.

I feel a pang of homesickness as I hug her goodbye, and it surprises me. I've been so focused on getting into Penn, on laying the groundwork for my own perfect future, that I didn't stop to think about how it would feel to leave. It's silly. I'm ninety minutes from home. They'll be back in a few weeks to take me to dinner, I'm sure. But still, this is it. I'll never live in their house as a child again.

They leave and I survey the disaster. Chloe's side of the room is perfect, naturally. She moved in this morning, her side unpacked and not a stray box to be seen. I flop onto her made bed and open a text message to Finn.

This is the first time I've had his phone number. Eric sent us a group text last week.

Everly, this is Finn's number. If you get arrested, use it.

Ha, ha, I'd written back.

And then Finn had typed, *If you have any questions about the campus, shoot me a message,* followed by a smiley face. That's an invitation, right?

I tap my bottom lip with my finger and think about what I should type. *Hey, Finn,* I start. *I'm all moved in.* I glance over at my mess. My things are in the room, so technically I'm not lying. *Do you have time to give me a campus tour?* I hit send.

I'm not completely nuts. I'm a freshman. He's a teacher. This will take some time. My expectations are set accordingly. We'll start with flirting. He'll see me as off limits at first. But I'll wear him down. I have four years. That's my plan. Freshman and sophomore years we'll establish a friendship. We'll date other people. I'll bide my time. By junior year he'll be thinking about me when he jerks off. Senior year, I'll make my move.

The door swings open and Chloe walks in, looking

triumphant.

"Everly! The library here is..." She puffs out a breath. "It's only a seven-minute walk!" I scoot over and she flops down onto the bed beside me. "What are you doing?"

"Waiting for Finn to text me back."

"Everly." She groans.

"What? It's perfectly appropriate for Finn to give me a tour of campus."

"Nothing in your head is appropriate."

My phone dings. We both lean over the screen and read it together. *Sure thing,* he's replied. *Which building are you in?*

Stroh Hall, I respond immediately.

I'll meet you out front tomorrow at 8 am and give you the walking tour. Make sure you know where the library is and where to find decent coffee during a midnight study session.

8 am? Now I'm the one groaning. There's no chance of stretching an 8 am meeting into a lunch. This guy is clueless.

See you at 8! I reply and roll off the bed. I toss my phone aside and dig into the bag with my sheets so I can get my bed sorted out.

"There are a lot of men in the world, Everly," Chloe says, watching me working. "Finn Camden is not the only guy out there."

"Of course he's not," I agree while securing the fitted sheet around the bottom corner of the mattress.

"But you're so convinced he's the one."

"The *right* one, yes."

"I don't see it, Everly." She says this softly, like it pains her to say it out loud. "I don't see how you two would make a good match, and I don't want you to miss out on the right guy because you're so fixated on Finn."

I finish with the fitted sheet and sit down. "But I'm not, Chloe. I dated Tim for two years and I dated Mark all summer. But they're just boys, you know? Long term, it's really important to choose wisely. I don't want to get it wrong and spend half my life shuttling kids back and forth to their fathers or dealing with my ex's new wife."

"Like my family?" Chloe says, and it's not a question, it's a statement. Her dad didn't even show up for graduation, too busy with his new family.

I nod. "Yeah, like that. And like seventy percent of our classmates. So if I choose wisely I can avoid a lot of heartache. I just have to be smart."

"That's a lofty goal, Everly Jensen."

I grin. "You know I love a challenge."

She nods. "Promise me one thing."

"Anything."

"Don't waste too much time chasing the wrong guy or you might miss the right one."

"Deal. If someone who is better for me than Finn Camden comes along, I'll give him a fair shot."

Nine

Present

"So we've established that you've been stalking Finn since you were six."

I shift in my seat and yank the sleeves of my sweater down to my fingertips. "I'm not sure anything I've done qualifies as stalking."

He slides an incredulous glance my way.

"Fine." I huff. "I'm not sure anything prior to the last year qualified as stalking."

"Better answer," he agrees. "So you've been following Finn's life," he says slowly, "in a friendly way, since you were a kid."

"He's my brother's best friend," I reply. "He was always just around. It's not like I was Googling him in grade school."

"Of course not," he agrees. But I suspect by the tone of his voice that he does think I was Googling Finn long before I was old enough to walk home from the bus stop unattended.

"Then you enrolled at the university that Finn just happened to be teaching at." He winks at me when he says this and it riles me up. "Thousands of higher education choices in this country, and you choose Penn."

"It's an Ivy League university, Sawyer," I snap. "There are only eight of those."

"Agreed. Well done."

He pauses and I feel smug in my defense.

"Where else did you apply?"

Fuck.

"Um, who can remember?" I stall and wind a strand of hair around my fingers. "College applications were so long ago, right?"

He nods, quiet for a moment. "I applied to Brown, Cornell and Harvard. I was accepted to all three. I ended up at Harvard because they had the best rowing program."

Damn. Of course he's a rower. I have a bit of a thing for rowers. Sophomore year I dated two of them. Not at the same time or anything. But still, it was a good year.

"And as you pointed out, I've got a few years on you."

"A decade."

"It's twelve years, if accuracy is important to you, Everly."

It's not. I'm just stalling and he knows it.

"So?" he prods.

I give up. I don't know how, but this guy has had my number since the moment we met. "Just Penn," I admit. Penn is the only place I applied. I drop the hair I've been twirling. "You wouldn't believe what I went through to get in though. I worked my ass off."

"I'm impressed."

This statement surprises me. I look at his face. He's sincere. "Why?" The question slips out of my mouth before I realize I'm speaking. Why should I care what he thinks? Yet I'm interested despite myself. And the rowing. Why did he have to mention the rowing? Now I'm checking him out. I can't make out too much under his blazer. It's a nice coat. A charcoal wool he's wearing over a white button-down and dark jeans. But the blazer is well made. Fitted. Likely custom based on the quality and the small amount of information I've gathered on this man. But I can see enough to know he's still in great shape under that jacket. Not that I care.

"I'm impressed at your tenacity. You set a goal and you achieved it."

"My goal is Finn," I remind him.

"Everly, we've already established that you haven't been

holding out exclusively for Professor Camden," he says, his lip twitching. "Which tells me that while you envision him as the perfect man, you've kept your options open. It tells me that while you might have a vivid fantasy of the perfect happily ever after, you're open"—he checks my response—"reluctantly, to being swept off your feet by someone other than Finn."

Well. I don't know how to respond to that, so what comes out of my mouth is, "Maybe I'm just a nymphomaniac."

This car ride just went from bad to worse.

"If you were a nymphomaniac you'd have given me a blowjob fifty miles ago."

"True," I agree. Damn it! I just said that out loud. I bite my lip and side-eye him. He's wearing a very satisfied smile.

Ten

Last Month

"Let's go!" I announce as I barge into Sophie's dorm room. Sophie is my other best friend. We met two years ago when I started working at Grind Me, a coffee bar just off campus, and we forged an instant friendship.

"Where are we going?" she asks.

She knows exactly where we're going. You make a girl a waxing appointment and they suddenly get amnesia. "You know where we're going, Sophie. Your pubes are not going to wax themselves."

"Please never say the word 'pubes' again," she says, but I ignore her. A good waxer is a godsend. She'll thank me later.

We exit her dorm and catch a bus at the nearest university bus stop. It's a beautiful afternoon in Philadelphia. The air has that crisp fresh smell that only comes with fall. We find seats on the bus and I grin at Sophie. "Are you nervous?"

"Yes! I told you I'm really not sure about this."

"Not about the waxing, nerd. Are you nervous about tomorrow?"

"Oh." She bites her lip and thinks. "Not really."

Sophie is finally going to have sex tomorrow, hence our trip to the waxing salon. This girl has picked some real winners, but her current boyfriend Mike is a nice guy. I don't think I'm wrong about him. He's a bit of a spoiled rich kid, but he's cute and he's really into Sophie.

"What are you doing this weekend?" Sophie asks me as my phone beeps.

"Going home." I frown at my screen. "My brother is getting married."

"Oh! That sounds fun. Are you taking the train?"

"I better not be taking the train." I hit send on a new message.

"Is someone driving down to pick you up?"

"No." I cross my legs and rest the phone on my thigh. "Professor Camden is driving me home."

"Really?" The doubt is written all over Sophie's face. "Professor Camden is driving you to Connecticut?"

I open my mouth to respond as my phone rings. I glance at the screen and smirk before breaking into a huge smile. "Yes, he is." I bring the phone to my ear and answer, "Yes, Professor Camden?" in my sweet and innocent voice. It doesn't get used a lot.

He lectures me about scheming and threatens to tell my brother why he should not drive me home for the wedding before finally agreeing, as I knew he would. I'm feeling pretty good when I tell him I'll be ready by eight, but then he ruins everything by asking me which dorm I live in. He should have such simple details about me memorized already. I sigh as I remind him that I live in Stroh and end the call to find Sophie looking at me with a face full of questions.

"Finn Camden is my brother's best friend. He's also the best man in his wedding this weekend." I shove the cell into my pocket. "He doesn't want to drive me home, so I texted my brother and told him I was going to take the train into New York City and then out to Connecticut. At night. By myself." I shrug. "Obviously the train is perfectly safe, but why should I take the train when Finn is going to the same place?" I can't believe Finn was going to let me take the train. It's disheartening, really. "I knew I could count on Eric to tell Finn to give me a ride home and that Finn couldn't bring himself to tell my brother that he doesn't want to be stuck in a car alone with me due to my"—I pause and roll my eyes—

"inappropriate advances."

"Wow." Sophie looks a little shocked.

"Right? He's being ridiculous. I don't have that much time left."

"Time?"

"Yeah. We graduate in seven months. I don't have any reason to stay in Philly after that. This is the optimal time window in which to make him fall in love with me." I pause, thinking. "Honestly, I could not have timed my brother's wedding any better. It's happening at the perfect time for me to advance my seduction of Finn."

"Um."

"He's finally single," I continue on. "I need him to accept us before he finds someone else and I graduate."

"Accept you?"

"That last girlfriend, just no." I shake my head. "He has no idea how much he's going to appreciate me in comparison. I guess I should thank her for that. But I won't."

Sophie crosses her legs and leans back on the bench seat. "Well, if anyone has the ability to force someone to fall in love with them, it'd be you, Everly Jensen."

Three Weeks Ago

I survey the table. Perfect. Everything is set for dinner. Finn's teaching a freshman-level Economics class right now, but he should be home just a few minutes after the lasagna is done. He loves lasagna. When he was a teenager he used to love staying over for dinner when my mom made lasagna, so I nabbed her recipe when I was home last month for my brother's wedding.

So the table is set and Mom's lasagna is in the oven. Laundry's done and put away. And Steve, our new pet, is happily swimming in his bowl. Steve's a big fat goldfish. I wanted to get a cat, but I'm not sure Finn's apartment allows pets. Plus, a cat is really something we should decide on together as a couple. But a goldfish is a nice start. I've placed him in the center of the table, kinda like a centerpiece. It's a little weird, maybe, but I thought he'd make a nice conversation piece over dinner. Finn can help me decide where his bowl should go permanently when he gets home.

Now it's time to make sure my housewife look is perfect too. I grab my bag and head into Finn's bathroom. I cleaned that earlier, while the sheets were in the wash. Honestly, I'm so good to him. I pull out the retro apron I ordered on Etsy and tie it around my waist, over my sweater and jeans. The pink and white polka-dot sash is long enough to wrap around my waist and then tie in the front. The vintage floral print below the sash hangs in an A-line style and ends a few inches above my knees.

My hair naturally lends itself to the look I'm going for today. It's thick and almost black and I've styled it with extra volume and huge side swept bangs, like a picture I found of Bridget Bardot. Next, makeup. I freshen up my face powder and reapply my lipstick. It's light pink, to match my nails. I know it seems like I'd go for red, but I'm going for a retro sweetheart look today. Plus, I found the perfect pink nail polish to coordinate. I spent forever at the beauty store going through all the pinks. You know how they name the colors? The wrong name can ruin everything. I'm sure of it. So while I liked the shade of Suzi Shops & Island Hops, the name was all wrong. But then I found a pink called Mod About You. Perfect, right? It really sets the tone for the evening.

Next I concentrate on my eyes. I watched a video on YouTube to get it just right, and I copy the look now, exaggerating the black eyeliner over my upper lid, into the perfect 1950's sex kitten.

I stash all my junk back into my bag and check on the lasagna. It's a lot of work making lasagna. I can't say it's my thing really, but for Finn, it's worth it. I've spent two weeks' worth of spending money on groceries and the perfect outfit for this evening.

I sigh in contentment. Everything's perfect. I'm graduating in the spring and real life is about to start, exactly like I always planned it.

The lock in the door turns and I blow out a breath as the door swings open, then plaster a sexy smile on my face.

Finn walks in and he can't miss me. His step falters for a minute, and I think he must be blown away by all the effort I've put into this and my smile widens.

Then he closes the door behind him and sags against it.

"Everly, how in the hell did you get in my apartment?"

Twelve

Present

"Do you enjoy cooking, Everly?"

"I live in a dorm room. I enjoy making microwave popcorn." This guy and his getting-to-know-me agenda has no end in sight. "And just so you know, asking a woman you're trying to seduce if she likes to cook is stupid."

"I love a good homemade lasagna myself," he says. "I can't remember the last time anyone made me lasagna though. It's a lot of work."

Oh. My. God. I feel my face flush with humiliation and I drop my head into my hand. "He told you about that?" I ask from behind my hand.

"Of course," he replies. "Called me the second he kicked you out."

I groan.

"That was a bold move on your part."

"It was crazy."

"Spirited."

I sigh and look out the passenger window. Breaking into Finn's apartment and making dinner did not go as I planned. Oh, I planned on him kicking me out, and he did. But he didn't even keep Steve. I mean, who can't keep a goldfish?

This entire fall has been a disaster, really. Starting with the car ride home from my brother's wedding. I tried to sex-talk Finn in the car and he turned on the radio. But I'm an aggressive girl and Finn's shy so I didn't let it phase me. Nope. Instead I placed my hand on his thigh, and as I started to slide it up his leg, Finn finally spoke.

He said no.

No, Everly. I deflate just thinking of it. *No, Everly, just no.*

I snatched my hand back, mortified. I'd never been turned down before. In my experience guys have enjoyed being pursued. Appreciated it, even. Maybe it would be nice to let the guy make the first move, but there's a lot of competition for the good ones. If you don't get aggressive and make things happen, some other girl snaps him up while you're sitting around waiting for an invitation. It's exhausting. And sure, it would be nice to be wooed, but it's not realistic. Especially in college. These boys are lazy.

So Finn shocked me speechless when he rejected me in the car. But then he glanced at me and smiled. "You're like a sister to me, Everly."

"I'm not your sister," I quickly interjected, and he just shook his head, saying it was against university policy. "You're not *my* teacher," I argued, desperate for a lifeline. But he just said it was a bad idea and ended the conversation.

Any other girl would have given up then. But not me. I'm not a quitter. I was prepared to wait until the spring semester to make my next move, but then I stopped by his office to find his trampy teaching assistant perched on his desk and I had to restrategize. There's no way I'm letting her sink her troll claws into him. Not on my watch.

So I used one of the keys I'd had made during my brother's wedding weekend to break into his apartment a few weeks ago. I'd made three copies of his house key when he'd asked me to move his car during the rehearsal dinner. I mean, who wouldn't? There was a hardware store right across the street. It seemed like fate, don't you think? And I swear Finn winked at me when he asked me to move his car. I swear it. So I moved the car and made three copies of his house key. Because I assumed he'd know I'd made multiple copies. What kind of an idiot steals someone's keys and only makes one copy?

But… he only asked for his *key* back. I remember standing in his hallway in shock. I'd had it all planned out. He'd smile at me and ask for the keys back. I'd give him two copies but I'd still have the third for the next time I wanted to break in. But it never even occurred to him that I'd made more than one copy. It was like he didn't know me at all.

I stood there, alone in the hallway, befuddled and questioning everything, when the door swung back open. My hopes lifted.

Then he shoved the goldfish bowl into my hands and said, "Take this with you."

I was halfway through saying, "His name is Steve," when the door shut in my face.

Do you have any idea how hard it is to walk home carrying a goldfish bowl? I mean, I got him there in one of those plastic bags filled with water that they sell them to you in. But I didn't have the bag anymore. Just Steve sloshing around in his bowl, judging me.

"I think you showed remarkable restraint," Sawyer says, pulling me out of my thoughts.

I shift in my seat and take a good look at him. "You do?"

"Absolutely. You could have shown up with a kitten. Or a dog."

"I thought about it," I admit, examining my manicure. My nails are painted Sole Mate purple. I selected the color in anticipation of bumping into Finn this weekend. "But I wasn't sure his apartment allowed pets."

"See, you're always thinking, Everly. I like that about you."

I shrug. "Can we be done talking now?"

"Oh, did you want your phone back?"

"Yes." I turn my head. "Can I have it?" Maybe he's finally going to shut up.

"Nope."

I groan and flop back in my seat while he laughs.

"I can't believe Finn didn't ask for the rest of the keys back."

"What?" That's got my attention. How could he possibly

know about the keys?

"When Finn called me I asked him if he'd gotten the keys back. He said, yeah, he got his *key* back, but I insisted you'd made more than one. I said, 'Finn, trust me on this. That girl'"—he winks at me, like he totally gets it—"'Everly would have made more than one copy.'" He glances at my face a beat. "My money's on three."

Thirteen

Four hours ago

"The game starts in ten minutes!" Dad says before taking a bite of his infamous leftover turkey sandwich. It's a concoction of turkey, stuffing and cranberry sauce on toasted bread and he looks forward to it all year long.

"Are we watching the Eagles or the Giants today?" I ask as the front door swings open and my brother Eric walks in with his new wife Erin. They've been married just under a month and they're perfect together, just like my parents.

He met her two years ago on a flight to Chicago. Yup, the whole 'sat on a plane next to each other and fell in love' scenario. He was traveling on business. She was traveling to attend a bridal shower for a friend. Three months later he was her date to that friend's wedding. Six months after that they were engaged themselves.

Our parents adore her. Everyone adores her, myself included. Eric and Erin just fit together. Like two peas in a pod. Peanut butter and jelly. Two halves of a whole. You get the idea. We've all seen that couple. Solid. Supportive. Their relationship reminds me of my parents'. Totally in sync. I want that too. And Finn Camden is a perfect fit. Steady. Reliable. He's a forever kind of guy.

Eric greets me with, "Hey, trouble," before noticing Dad's sandwich and making a dive for the other half.

"We got the wedding photos back." Erin's clutching a giant

album to her chest. "Your mom wanted to go over them with us."

"With you, honey," Eric interrupts. "That's a wife job. No one needs me for this."

"A wife job?" I ask, brow raised. But Eric and Erin just exchange smiles while I utter, "Never mind, I don't even want to know."

"You girls have fun. I'm going to Finn's to catch up. Call me when you're ready, babe."

"Wait!" I call out and Eric stops, Dad's sandwich rapidly disappearing into his mouth. "You're going to Finn's?" This is my opportunity. I gotta admit, things really have a way of working out for me. "Finn's giving me a ride back to school," I tell him. "I'll catch a ride with you and save him a trip over here."

"He is?" Eric questions, but he's not really paying attention to me—he's distracted watching his new wife tuck a strand of hair behind her ear.

Finn has no idea he's driving me back to school, but I say, "Yes," all the same. "Just give me a second to grab my stuff."

I dash upstairs and whip off the sweatshirt I'm wearing and pull on a cream-colored cashmere sweater. My brown knee-high boots will look great with this. I freshen my lipstick and say a silent thank you to the heavens for giving me the foresight to do my hair this morning. It's normally fairly straight and shiny all on its own, but I flat-ironed it to perfection instead of a ponytail.

I toss everything I brought home for the Thanksgiving holiday into my bag and then sit on the bed to tug on the boots. It crosses my mind that I have no plan in place. That Finn hasn't agreed to drive me back to school, has no idea I'm about to show up with Eric as if he's already offered a ride. But I dismiss it. Like I said, things usually work out, and a positive attitude is essential. Plus, Finn is too much of a gentleman to humiliate me in front of my brother. That's how he got stuck driving me to and from the wedding last month.

Still, the indignity of getting tossed out of his apartment

just a few weeks ago is fresh on my mind. But so is that tramp teaching assistant I've seen eyeing him.

I hesitate, bag in hand. Maybe I shouldn't push it. But then again, we're friends, at the very least. Right? There's no reason he can't give me a ride back to campus. We're both going to the same place, after all. In fact, it's economical for him to drive me. And environmentally friendly. I nod my head. I've always been concerned about the environment.

So he'll drive me back. I'll be normal. I won't make one inappropriate advance. We'll laugh. He'll drop me off and realize he wants to spend more time with me. I've totally got this.

Fourteen

Three Hours Ago

I've never been to Finn Camden's house before. My knee bounces in anticipation while I sit in the passenger seat of Eric's car. Finn is eight years older than me, and Finn was Eric's friend, so obviously there was never a reason for me to go to Finn's house. I'm curious to see it. Finn hasn't lived there for years now, but it'll be something to add to my mental Finn file.

We turn right onto North Road, after passing the Venice Restaurant and Pizzeria, and I laugh.

"What's funny?" Eric asks.

"Remember how Dad always ordered clams on his pizza and no one would touch it but him?"

"Disgusting," Eric agrees, but he's smiling. "And Mom would order pepperoni for the rest of us."

"Yeah."

"I should take Erin," he muses while we wait for a light to change.

"You should," I agree.

"What about you, Everly?"

"What about me what?" I ask, confused.

"Are you seeing anyone?" He looks over at me. "At school?"

Not successfully, I think to myself. "No, not right now. I'm kinda taking a break this semester."

"Taking a break," Eric repeats, glancing over at me. "That's not like you. At all."

I shrug. "It's exhausting."

"What's exhausting?" he asks, frowning.

"Um—" *Breaking and entering,* I think. But I can't tell him that. "You know, the whole 'does he like me' thing."

"If you have to wonder if a guy likes you, then he's not the right guy for you, Everly."

"Maybe it's more complicated than that."

"It's never more complicated than that."

I nod, not because I agree, but because there's really nothing more I can say. Thankfully we're pulling into a driveway on Ridgebury, so I'm saved from having to discuss it further.

The landscaping is gorgeous, even this late into fall. Huge pine trees line the drive and a towering birch tree sits in the middle of an island created by the circular drive. The leaves have partially fallen away, and I can see that the tree clears the two-story house. I know the houses over here have been here for decades, so I'm not sure if the tree was planted with the house, or if the driveway was created around the tree in order to preserve it.

Based on the drive in, it appears that all the homes on this street sit on a few acres each. It's idyllic. I'm surprised I ever saw Eric and Finn at my house. I'd have hung out here every chance I got.

There are several cars in the drive, and I spot Finn's among them. Eric parks and we're heading for the front door when I remember Finn has no idea I'm coming. I bite my lip and say a quick prayer that this works out.

The front door is flanked by glass panels and a big yellow dog watches us approach. He lets out a laid-back bark in greeting and the door is swung open by a woman I'm guessing is Finn's mother. She gives Eric a hug while the dog nudges my hand and looks at me hopefully. I bend down to scratch his head and he falls to the floor, rolls onto his back and thumps his tail. I laugh and rub his belly instead.

Eric introduces me to Mrs. Camden and I stand politely while she asks about his recent wedding. I glance around the foyer while they talk, admiring the inside of the home. It's about what I'd assumed—nice. I know from my prying over the years that Finn's dad is a lawyer and his mom is an interior designer. The house shows it, for sure. It looks like the pages of a home magazine, yet lived in. The dog at my feet is proof that a family lives here and it's more than a showpiece.

I turn my attention to Mrs. Camden. I'd estimate her to be a few years older than my parents, maybe early to mid-sixties. She looks very chic wearing a crisp white blouse tucked into dark jeans, a belt looped around her trim waist. She's formal, yet approachable, much like the house.

"You're a student at Penn, correct, Everly?" She's finished exchanging pleasantries with Eric and has turned to me.

I nod. "I am. For a few more months. I'm a senior."

"What are your plans after graduation?" She looks so genuinely interested in my response that I feel like a heel. I don't have any plans, other than Finn. The truth is, I'm floundering. Graduation is around the corner and I'm not entirely sure what I want to do with the rest of my life. My friends are all so confident in their intended career paths, lining up internships and interviews, researching apartments and choosing roommates. And me? I'm breaking into Finn's apartment.

"I'm not sure yet." I smile and wave it off like it's not a big deal.

She nods as a chorus of objections float down the hallway and the dog perks up from his spot on the floor and trots off to investigate.

"They're watching the game," Mrs. Camden tells us and gestures to where the dog disappeared to. "They're in the den. Head on back."

I follow Eric through the wide entry hall towards the back of the house. We enter a large kitchen, an assortment of snacks out on the marble-covered island. The kitchen has a wall of windows showcasing the backyard and a set of French doors that open onto a paved patio. There's a large in-ground pool, covered for the season, in the yard beyond the patio, complete with a pool house of some sort. The landscaping in the back is no less impressive than the front. The pots on the patio are filled with seasonal plantings and the yard is filled strategically with towering maple and pine trees.

Eric continues to the right, a short wide hallway emptying into the den. He strides in, confident on his path, as I trail behind and assess my game plan.

But any game plan I can conjure is pointless in the end. Because everything is about to change.

Fifteen

Three Hours Ago

Finn is on the couch, his focus on the television as we enter the room. But he's not alone. And he's not watching the game with his father, as I'd assumed. There's another man on the couch with him. A few years older, maybe. A bit darker, surely. Their body types are nothing alike. Whereas Finn has a lanky runner's physique, this man is built in an entirely different way. Fit, most definitely. But stronger. He must have twenty pounds on Finn, all of it muscle across a broader chest and a taller frame.

This other man notices us immediately and his eyes run over me and spark with an interest I'm familiar with. An interest I'm always searching for in Finn and never finding, no matter how aggressively I push for it.

Finn is a moment behind in noticing us and he deflates a little when he sees me. I hate to admit it, but it's true. I can see that now. The difference in reaction between Finn and this other man is so discernible when I can analyze them simultaneously.

The moment is over in a heartbeat, Eric calling out a greeting that has them rising from the couch, and then they're all clapping each other on the back in that way that men do. There's a pause then, a moment so brief I know I'm the only one catching it, as the man looks between Eric and me, quickly analyzing our body language, the shade of our hair, the similarity in our features, and correctly assessing who I am, the same way I've assessed him. Recognition crosses his face and his eyes land on mine with amusement and a hint of fascination.

"You're Eric's little sister."

A lifetime of etiquette forces me to nod and step forward. "Yes," I say, reaching out a hand to shake. "I'm Everly."

"You two haven't met, have you?" Eric notes as the man grasps my hand. Sparks do not fly. Chills do not run through my body. I do not suddenly recognize this man as my soulmate based on a handshake. Such bullshit. His hand is nice though. Firm, large. His thumb caresses the back of my hand and fine, that touch alone is enough to make me recognize that he's probably good in bed. But that's it.

"No, we haven't," I agree, as I wonder why I've never given this man a moment's thought before now. I've known of his existence, certainly. My mind flips through every reference Finn has made to him throughout the years. I just haven't cared, I suppose. He had nothing to do with my Finn Camden agenda and was thus irrelevant.

"I'm Sawyer," the man says. "Finn's brother."

I've figured this out for myself, of course. Just as he's determined I'm Eric's sister. It wasn't any similarity between Finn and Sawyer that gave it away. It was simply the way he belonged here. An arm across the back of the couch, legs sprawled before him. Confident. Relaxed. Lounging on this couch, in this room, a mundane event.

"What's the score?" Eric asks, grabbing a seat on the sofa.

"Twenty-one to seventeen, Giants lead," Finn responds and drops back on the couch on the other side of Eric.

I'm still standing, Sawyer beside me. I eye the spot Sawyer vacated when he stood, next to Finn, but make a quick judgment that it would be weird if I took Sawyer's spot, so I take a seat on the huge sectional in a spot where I can see Finn instead.

Sawyer sits beside me.

I can't discreetly glimpse at Finn with Sawyer between us.

He's already on my nerves.

Eric and Finn jump right into conversation, interrupting themselves to make commentary on the game. I glance over at them a few times and realize that Sawyer is watching me. His spot on the sofa puts me between him and the television, so it looks like he's watching the game, but he's not. He's watching me. He's not even hiding it. Every glance I make back towards Eric and Finn, I catch him, if you can catch someone who isn't attempting to hide. I meet his gaze and give him a snarky look, one I've perfected with men that says, *I see you staring at me, asshole.*

He laughs.

The sound catches Eric's attention and reminds him I'm in the room, his head snapping over to me. "You guys don't need to leave before the game's over, do you?" he asks, glancing between me and Finn.

Finn looks bewildered by Eric's question. Then realization dawns and he rubs the back of his neck and shakes his head slightly. "Everly..."

I'm not sure what he's about to say, but whatever it is, it's not going to end well for me, I know that much. I open my mouth to say something, anything, to defuse the situation but I don't get a word out because Sawyer interrupts before I get the chance.

"Finn's not headed back to Philadelphia until tomorrow morning," he says.

Oh. The second the words are out of his mouth I remember that Finn doesn't teach an early class on Mondays. Why didn't I think of that when I hatched this plan to drop in and get a ride back to school? I almost groan out loud. What a rookie mistake. "Well," I begin, but Sawyer interrupts again.

"I'm heading back to Philadelphia right now. I'll be happy to drive you."

Of course he will.

I want to kill this guy. Instead, I stall. "You live in Philadelphia?" I ask, turning my head towards him.

He's still looking at me, of course, his eyes making a slow

survey of my face.

"I do," he says.

"I'm sure it would be out of your way to drop me off on campus," I say with a stiff smile, staring back at him.

"It wouldn't be," he answers, the corner of his mouth twitching.

Finn is already nodding his head, a relieved smile on his face. "Perfect. Sawyer will drive you back."

My brother frowns, looking from Sawyer to me, but keeps his mouth shut.

I stand, defeated. I straighten my sweater over the waistband of my leggings and look towards the doorway, stating I'll grab my things from Eric's car.

"She's twenty-two, Sawyer," my brother says as soon as he thinks I'm out of earshot. I roll my eyes and keep walking. He's wasting his breath. Sawyer Camden is of zero interest to me. None whatsoever.

Sixteen

Three Hours Ago

I step outside and slip my phone out of my pocket as I walk to Eric's car to retrieve my bag. I type out a quick text to my roommate Chloe as I walk. *You'll be happy to know my latest Finn Camden scheme has just tanked. Epically.*

Delighted. Her reply is quick and I smile. Chloe would never dare pull the stunts I do. She's a habitual rule-follower. A text bubble on my phone indicates she is typing again and then, *Dare I ask?* appears on my screen.

My scheming just landed me a car ride back to Philly with Finn's asshole brother, I type, smiling as I lean against the car.

Oh, a brother… I'm intrigued.

Don't be, I type.

The front door shuts and I glance up to find Sawyer walking towards me. He's attractive, I'll give him that. If you go for tall, incredibly fit men with chiseled jaws and thick dark hair. Which no girl does, ever. It must suck to be him.

He grabs my stuff and leads me to a small silvery blue sports car—a Porsche, I note with a roll of my eyes. He holds the passenger door open for me before tossing my bag in the trunk.

I slide into the passenger seat of the low-slung car as the door thuds shut behind me and busy myself with the seatbelt, using the opportunity to watch him as he crosses the front of the car. His strides are confident, unhurried. The fingers of his left hand skim the hood before he rounds the headlight and reaches the driver's side door.

I suddenly feel uneasy, and I never feel uneasy.

This car is too small for the both of us. I'm annoyed at the idea of being cooped up inside the same ten square feet as him all the way to Philadelphia. I just met him twenty minutes ago. Why is he having this effect on me?

The door handle clicks and he's behind the wheel, the engine purring a second later. I watch him buckle himself in from the corner of my eye, but keep my head straight, my focus on my hands folded in my lap, until the silence goes on too long. He's staring at me, the car idling, apparently content to wait until he has my attention. I turn my head and meet his eyes. They're brown, another check mark completing tall, dark and handsome. They light up with amusement as he speaks, which unsettles me. Why?

"How can you possibly think Finn Camden is the right man for you?"

That's why.

Seventeen

Present

We exit the interstate at 30th Street and I sigh in relief. We're less than two miles from my dorm. This car ride is almost over.

"Did you just sigh at me?" Sawyer asks as he merges the car into traffic.

"Yes. You're exhausting."

"Not used to this level of attention, Boots?"

I snort and lean against the door so I can watch him.

"Do you prefer to be in charge?" We're sitting at a stoplight and he turns to examine me. "Do you prefer to do the chasing? Or are you happy dating boys you have to pursue?"

I shrug. "They were just practice for Finn. What does it matter?"

He's shaking his head before I'm even finished speaking. "This idea you have of being with my brother, it's never happening. He's not right for you, you must know that."

"Why not? Why is it such a bad idea? Finn's a great guy. He's my brother's best friend. My parents already love him. And he's hot." I know it's a bitchy move to throw that in but Sawyer just nods in response.

"No chemistry."

"We have chemistry."

"You know that you don't."

"Well—" I pause. "It's only because he won't give it a

chance." I know this is a weak argument, but I don't want to give in.

"You overwhelm him, Everly. You're a whirlwind, and Finn, he's not an aggressive guy. You'd steamroll his life and end up disappointed by his lack of intensity."

"You know this from spending three hours with me?"

"I do," he says, looking me in the eye. "How can you not?"

I break his gaze and look out the window. I'm a lot to handle, I know that. But I never thought of it like that before.

"When's the last time someone asked you on a date, Boots?"

Wow. The hits just keep on coming with this guy. "I do okay." Does he think I'm chasing Finn because nobody else is interested?

"No. When's the last time a man pursued you? Instead of the other way around?"

"It doesn't work that way any more, Sawyer. My generation is different than yours." Ha.

He ignores the dig. "Any man worthy of you would work for it, Everly. Not sit by passively while you did all the work."

I don't have a single smart retort for that.

We arrive in front of my dorm and I pop the door open the second the car stops moving. I can't get my feet on the pavement fast enough. Sawyer puts the car in park and retrieves my bag from the trunk, walking around the car to hand it to me. I sling the bag over my shoulder and look up at him expectantly, hand out. He's standing so close I have to tilt my head back a little to meet his eyes.

"Phone?" I demand.

"Keys?" he replies.

Grrr. I dig into my bag and pull out the remaining two keys to Finn's apartment and drop them in his hand, then go back to looking at him expectantly, hand out.

"Don't you want to thank me for the ride, Everly?"

Right. Of course. I drop my outstretched hand and take a deep breath. It's better than a sigh. Not much, but I'm trying. "Thank you for driving me back to school, Sawyer. I appreciate it." I add on a smile. "May I have my phone now?"

Sawyer just continues to stand there and look at me, his eyes doing that thing again, that thing that makes me think he's picturing me naked. I do sigh now, and reach into his breast pocket and grab the phone myself.

"Is this you passively giving me my phone back? To prove how annoying it—"

I'm cut off mid-sentence because Sawyer's lips are on mine. One hand is behind my neck, warm on my skin and holding me still. The other is low on my hip, dangerously close to my ass, pulling me closer. My heart stops for a second, and then it's racing, blood flowing at warp speed throughout my body. I'm clutching my phone, my arm trapped between our bodies and across his chest. His tongue dips into my mouth and he groans. My traitorous ears are quick to acknowledge it's the sexiest thing I've ever heard, that this kiss, God, this kiss...

"That's chemistry," he says when he lets me go. I'm a few seconds behind hearing him, my eyes still closed, my lips still tilted in his direction.

Then his words register. I blink and take a step back. I just, I just don't have anything to say to that. I need to think. I whirl around and make a getaway for the dorm entrance, intent on getting out of there without giving him another look.

"Boots!" he shouts at me as I dash up the steps, door in sight.

"What?" I snap, stopping at the top of the steps and turning to look at him again.

"So I'll call you?" he asks, smiling. "We can Netflix and chill?" He laughs as he says it, leaning against the car with his hands in his pockets.

"You're an asshole, Sawyer! And you're at least a decade too old to be using that phrase!"

He must find rejection funny because he's still laughing as I yank open the building door and disappear inside.

Chloe is dunking a tea bag into a mug of hot water from the small microwave in our room when I get upstairs. I drop my bag on the floor and flop face first onto my bed, burying my face in a pillow.

"Pfft!"

"What's that?" Chloe asks.

Her bed creaks and the covers rustle as she sits, so I roll over and suck in a breath. "He's impossible," I tell her, waving my hands in the general direction of the ceiling. "Impossible!"

"Who's that?" Chloe asks, smiling. She's sitting cross-legged on the bed facing me, her fingers wrapped around the steaming mug. "The brother?"

"Yes. *Him.*" I stress the word with all the disdain I can muster. "He's arrogant. And pushy! He manipulated me into accepting a ride back with him to Philly, took away my phone and forced me to talk with him the entire drive!"

Chloe blinks for a second and then the giggles start.

"What's funny?" I ask, swinging myself up to a sitting position and leaning against the wall. I'm failing to see how anything I said was funny.

Chloe, however, is laughing so hard she's had to set the mug down. "What's funny?" she repeats. "What's funny is that he's *you*, Everly."

I shake my head. "No, he's bossy."

Chloe snorts.

"Fine, I might be a little bossy, but he was intrusive. Super nosey. You should have heard the things he was asking me." I cross my arms across my chest and nod, waiting for her to agree.

"Everly, you signed me up for a dating site last semester. Without my knowledge."

Well, there's that. "I gave you plenty of opportunities to do it yourself first," I mutter.

"You sent me on a date, Everly. Without telling me I was on a date. I spent an hour with the guy before I figured out not only did he not need tutoring, he had, in fact, graduated three years ago."

"You were getting along so well online," I mumble.

"By which you mean he was getting along with *you* impersonating *me* online."

"Um." I examine my nails and avoid looking at her. "Well, the thing is, I expected that was going to end differently." I smile hopefully. "Also, I did that to help. I'm a helper." I shrug.

"That you are, my friend, that you are." She sips her tea and examines me over the rim. "So the brother—"

"Sawyer," I supply.

"Sawyer." She nods, committing it to memory. "Parents had a Mark Twain thing going on, huh?"

"Appears so," I agree, smiling. My mom would appreciate their literary baby-naming method.

"So the brother, Sawyer." She grins. "He sounds interesting." She raises a brow in question.

"No. He absolutely was not." I shoot her a dirty look. "No."

"Okay." She shrugs. "If you say so."

"I do."

"But Everly?" Her tone is serious.

"What?" I'm apprehensive.

"Remember, after we made our college decisions based on your"—she pauses and her lips twitch—"innovative plan to make Finn Camden fall in love with you, you promised me that you'd keep an open mind."

I nod.

"It's okay to rewrite your happily ever after, Everly. Sometimes the right guy is the one you never see coming."

Eighteen

"What's that?" I ask, pointing to the large shopping bag sitting on my bed when I return from class Monday afternoon.

Chloe looks up from her desk, tendrils of hair escaping the messy knot piled on her head. She drops the pen she's holding on the desk and turns her attention to me. "It was waiting for you downstairs. I brought it up on my way in."

I eye the package as I drop my backpack on the floor beside my bed, then slip out of my coat and toss it on my desk chair. Placing both hands on my hips, I stare at it some more.

"I'm assuming that guy, the one you're not interested in, sent it," Chloe comments from her desk, watching me with interest.

I shrug, then peer inside the bag. There's a box wrapped in plain white paper and a big orange bow, my favorite color. I smooth the ribbon under my fingers and wonder what Sawyer is up to, because she's right. I've never wandered into my room and found a Neiman Marcus bag waiting for me. There's a card attached to the ribbon that simply says, *For Boots.*

God, he's given me a nickname and he's sending me gifts. No one's ever given me a nickname before. Well, romantically anyway. Finn nicknamed me Shortcake when I was six, but that was different. None of the guys I dated ever called me anything but babe or baby, which is the worst. It's generic and kinda silly. I was always tempted to give a little infant wail in response, just to see what they'd have to say, but I never went through with it.

I tug the ribbon and it falls away, quickly followed by the paper. It's a Christian Louboutin box. Chloe is watching with interest as I open the lid. Holy shit. It's a pair of boots. The pair I've been admiring all fall, pinned to my fall wardrobe inspiration board on Pinterest. They're a combination of leather and suede with a three-inch stiletto heel, the zipper concealed along the back. Totally impractical and totally out of my price range. Way, way out of my price range. Which doesn't stop me from trying them on.

Remember the feeling you got when you were a little girl and slipped on your favorite princess dress? Stepping into a pair of Louboutins feels even better than that. Way, way better.

"You know you have to send them back," Chloe says, watching me check myself out in the mirror on the back of the door.

"Do I?" I say slowly. "I mean, isn't that the biggest cliché? Guy sends girl gift, girl fawns over the gift then insists she can't accept it? Where did such a ridiculous practice begin, anyway? It's quite stupid," I add, sitting down to take the boots off.

"You said you weren't interested in him, so you can't accept gifts from him. That's standard etiquette."

Etiquette. Only Chloe would etiquette-check a girl with a brand-new pair of Louboutins. I shake my head as I step out of my jeans before pulling on a grey cable-knit sweater dress. Chloe tilts her head and raises an eyebrow as I slip the boots back on and admire my new outfit combination.

"Ohh, they look good with a dress too. They're so versatile, Chloe! I can wear them with everything." I turn to face her, hand on hip, waiting for her commentary.

She shakes her head.

"It's rude to refuse a gift, Chloe." I'm sure I've heard that somewhere.

"In the south. That's only a thing in the south, Everly, and you are not southern."

I frown. How the hell did southern girls pull that off and why isn't it a universal thing? I sit at my desk and watch Steve swim in his bowl. "Do you think he's happy in there?" I ask, pointing a thumb at Steve. "Do you think he needs a little tank? Or a friend? That bowl is really small." I frown, worried I am failing at fish parenting.

"I think he's fine," she says and, giving up on talking sense into me, goes back to her studying.

I should study too. I tap my toes on the floor, admiring the boots from this vantage, and open up my laptop. I'll just take a quick peek at my Pinterest board first to see what else these boots would look good with. Everything. They look good with everything, I decide after a half hour of pinning. Which somehow ended with me pinning knitting patterns. I don't knit, but Pinterest is a bitch that way.

Chloe's right. I shouldn't keep the boots. I'm not interested in Sawyer. I'm not. I've spent a long time thinking Finn was the perfect guy for me, and I'm not ready to give up on that. Just because Sawyer can kiss—and okay, just because I'm attracted to him—doesn't make him the right one for me. Not for the long haul and that's what I'm interested in. I can't date them both. Once you date one brother, the other is off limits. For life. I don't even need Chloe telling me to know that.

I reach down and slip the boots off my feet, then carry them back to my bed where the box is. There's another card. I didn't notice it before, placed under the boots. I pick it up. It's a notecard, no envelope. The card stock is heavy and his name is embossed in gold print along the bottom, aligned to the right. Sawyer Camden.

I place the boots in the box and sit, running my index finger over the edge of the card for a moment. A note from Sawyer.

I like you.

That's it. That's what's written on the inside of the card, and it confuses me. Not the statement. I got that much in the car on Sunday. But my feelings confuse me. I'm so flustered by him. By his interest. By his certainty. By that kiss.

I run a finger over my bottom lip, remembering it, and flush. To be honest, I'm not completely sure what it meant to him. I mean, was he just fucking with me? Proving a point? Or did he mean it? I'm not sure. He's a thirty-four-year-old man. Successful, by the looks of his car, the assistant on speed dial. I'm a twenty-two-year-old college senior with a delusional one-sided thing for his brother. Why me?

Yet I can't discount the chemistry. He wasn't lying about that, there's most definitely *something* between us. But just because you're attracted to someone doesn't mean it's a good idea to act on it. The road to hell is paved with attractive men who radiate sex appeal and look like models from a Polo ad campaign.

Or something like that.

Nineteen

"He bought you an Elf on the Shelf?" I'm at work and my friend Sophie is catching me up on her Thanksgiving weekend. She spent it with her new boyfriend, the gynecologist. I think it's weird too, but he is crazy hot. And in her defense, she didn't know he was a gynecologist until she ended up in his exam room. But that's a story for another time.

"Yeah. Neither of us really knew what it was, but we looked it up and now he texts me pictures of the elf every morning," she says with a big grin.

"Pictures of the elf on his dick?" I ask hopefully. Because this domestic elf shit is just a little much.

"No! Pictures of the elf doing funny stuff around his house."

Huh. I don't know what to make of that.

"Never mind." She waves a hand to close the subject.

But still, I blurt out, "Holy shit. He's in love with you."

She demurs, insists they're just having fun, but Sophie is not a having-fun kind of girl. This can't possibly end well. That guy is all wrong for her.

"Okay, enough about me," she says. "Tell me about your weekend. Did you make any headway with Professor Camden?"

"I…" I start to answer her, but stop. "I don't know what is going on anymore, Sophie."

"What do you mean?" Sophie tilts her head in concern. "You always know what is going on. You have a plan, remember? Six months till graduation, six months to make Finn Camden fall in love with you."

As if I need reminding. "I know, I know, but I'm so confused." I can feel my face fall as I talk, my forehead creased in worry. Confused is an understatement.

"Is everything okay?"

"Yeah." I suck in a gulp of air and plaster a smile on my face. I'm not ready to talk about this with Sophie. I haven't even fully talked it out with Chloe. I told her I wasn't deviating from my Finn Camden plan and she just groaned and thumped her head on the desk.

I'm saved from thinking any more about the Finn versus Sawyer debacle that is currently my life because Sophie's stalker has just walked into the coffee shop. I point him out and get the usual lecture about the difference between a regular customer and a stalker. I barely have time to shrug before the guy is at the counter asking her out and then flashing a federal ID at her when she declines.

Knew it. Well, I didn't know that, exactly. But I knew he wasn't a customer. I snatch the ID up and examine it while Sophie shifts nervously and asks if she's in trouble.

The guy is extremely good-looking and, not gonna lie, the badge makes him that much hotter. Gallagher. Nice Irish name. I run my finger over the three-dimensional surface while I have one of my best ideas to date. "Feds aren't really her fetish, but I know a girl at school who'd be so into you," I blurt out, my mood instantly lifted.

"Everly!" Sophie and Agent Gallagher reply simultaneously with near-identical looks of exasperation.

Whatever. I have so many good ideas, but sometimes you just can't help people when they don't want to be helped.

A flower delivery arrives and I grin, looking forward to Sophie signing for a flower delivery from her boyfriend while this agent guy attempts to hit on her. It's the most stunning arrangement of flowers I've ever seen. A sea of orange blooms. I think I spot a peony. I love peonies. Luke and Sophie must have had one hell of a weekend. But then the delivery man looks up and asks for me.

I walk to the other end of the counter to get out of Sophie's way and accept the delivery. They're even more stunning up close. Roses, peonies, some miniature calla lilies in orange. An assortment of greenery. I'm not sure what it all is. The vase itself is at least a foot tall.

The delivery man places them on the counter and then pulls out his clipboard and frees a card from the clamp. It's not a business card-sized envelope, the kind that normally comes with a bouquet. It's a notecard. My name and work address at the coffee shop are typed across the front. He places it on the counter next to the flowers and wishes me a good day while I stand motionless and stare at it, deep in thought.

It's obviously from Sawyer. I lean on the back counter and stare at it from a safe three feet away. He's done his homework. The orange ribbon yesterday, the boots I've been coveting, the orange flowers today. That can't be a coincidence. He's looked, or had his assistant look—what was her name? Sandra. They've clearly looked at enough of my social profiles to send what I'd like. I don't think Sandra is responsible for more than the legwork here though. She wouldn't have known to send me boots in honor of the nickname he'd coined for me without him specifying to do so.

A customer arrives, interrupting my musings and procrastination over opening the envelope. Sophie's still busy with the agent so I move the flowers and card to the back counter and take their order. Two more customers file in and I busy myself with their orders, the unopened card never out of my consciousness, as much as I try to pretend I'm not curious about its contents.

I finish up with the customers then ponder making myself a drink. I get as far as filling the portafilter with espresso and leveling it before I admit to myself I will not wait another second to open the envelope. I abandon my drink-making and slide the envelope off the counter and run my finger under the glue on the back to break the seal. I slide the card out. It's the same as yesterday's. Heavy cream card stock with Sawyer

Camden written in a bold font along the bottom edge, off centered to the right. I flip it open.

I want you.

Like yesterday's note—*I like you*—this is all that is written on the card. Short. Effective, I'll admit, because it causes me to suck in my breath as desire winds its way through my body. I smile and stuff the card back into the envelope, then tap the card on the countertop.

Sawyer Camden, what in the hell am I going to do about you?

Twenty

I'm in class on Thursday when I receive a message from Chloe. *You have another delivery,* it reads.

He's persistent, I'll give him that. I peer over my open laptop at the professor, droning on. She's yet to say one thing worthy of notating. I've majored in Communications. Why? Because I have not one clue what I want to do with my life. Other than Economics—I know I don't want anything to do with that. I like people. I like communicating with them. And I can use a communications degree a lot of different ways. Maybe something in public relations. I do enjoy strategizing. Or event planning. Or social media management. I'd be great at that.

Is it a shoe box? I type back.

Definitely not a shoe box! Chloe's reply is quick.

Evasive much, Chloe?

All I receive in reply to that is a smiley face emoticon. I tap my fingers on the desk. She's not going to tell me what it is. I eye Professor Richland and contemplate ditching the rest of this class. But no. I'm not *that* interested in what Sawyer has sent. I'm not.

I close the message box and focus on the lecture. I eye the door, but this professor specializes in calling students out for arriving late or leaving early. I settle in and wait it out, sketching pictures in my notebook to pass the time.

By the time I get back to Stroh Hall Chloe has left for her next class. It gives me some satisfaction that she's not there to watch me open whatever this is, since she wouldn't give me any clues via message. I shut the door behind me and look at my bed, expecting to see a package. Nada. I glance around the room. Then I see it on my desk. A tiny fish tank. Steve's bowl is gone and in its place is a fish tank, already set up and running.

I sink down onto my desk chair and take it in. He's sent a fish tank for Steve. And... a friend, I note, seeing a second fish in the tank. This one's got some white on its fins, which will be helpful in telling them apart. I tap on the side of the glass and Steve waves his little fish fin at me while blowing bubble kisses. No, not really. He's a fish, and they do absolutely nothing. I unscrew the lid to the goldfish and drop a few flakes in. That gets their attention.

In any case, Steve must be pleased with his new home and I have to admit it's nice. It's not a large tank, not taking up much more room than the bowl, but it looks pretty fancy for being so small. There's a light and a little rock formation they can swim through. The pamphlet lying on my desk next to it proclaims it to be a self-cleaning system. Nice. There's a card, of course, propped up next to the tank.

Her name is Stella, it reads.

I laugh then. This guy, he's... I don't know. He's not what I expected. I wonder if he puts this much effort into all his conquests. And then I wonder what that might be like, being with Sawyer. His attention to detail, putting this much effort into seducing me, makes me suspect he'd be just as attentive in the bedroom. Or hallway. Car. Whatever. But he's clearly done this before. Maybe not a fish, or boots specifically. But he's got twelve years on me. It makes me wonder. And not in a 'how many women has he slept with' kind of way. But in a 'how many women have mattered' kind of way. Is this status quo seducing for Sawyer Camden? I want to punch myself in the face for being so cliché, but am I special? Or am I a challenge? Maybe he's just doing Finn a favor by taking me off his hands. Not that Finn ever had his hands on me.

But yet I know that's not true. There is something between

us, something more than desire. Sawyer challenges me, in a sort of terrifying way. In the car, he laughed at all of those crazy stories, and he always seems to be two steps ahead of me. It's exhilarating. Usually people are trying to rein me in, not encourage me, but I don't think Sawyer would. I think instead of wanting me to tone it down, he'd look forward to what I'd throw at him next.

Twenty-One

I wake on Friday more confused than ever. I slept fitfully, having had a strange dream about Sawyer. And Finn. Even my childhood sweetheart Tim Stuart made an appearance. He was full grown in the dream, but still sporting the haircut I gave him when we were six.

I dreamt that I married Tim. In my dream we lived in our hometown of Ridgefield, Connecticut and paid for everything with green Skittles. It was one of those awful dreams that feel as if they're going on for hours, even though scientists will insist they last just minutes.

We went to the local pizzeria, Venice, and while Tim was counting out green Skittles to pay the bill I looked up to see Finn. He was there with a woman. She was no one I recognized. I felt relief that it wasn't that graduate student I detest, the one who's been eyeing him for months, but nothing beyond that. They looked good together, happy, and I didn't feel much but a casual curiosity to see who he ended up with.

Then Sawyer walked in with a woman, and the dream took a decidedly different tone. His arm was resting on her lower back in an intimate way, guiding her to Finn's table, and I felt like I got punched in the gut. Tim asked me what was wrong, so I shoved a handful of non-green Skittles into my mouth to avoid answering him, which annoyed him greatly. Apparently we used the yellow Skittles to start the car. None of it made any sense. Dreams are so stupid.

Yet I can't shake that it means something. It plagues me all morning. While I shower and dress. While I blow my dark hair into straight glossy perfection and paint my nails in the color A Good Man-darin is Hard to Find.

So when I finish with my afternoon class I walk over to the Hymer building, where Finn's office is. I need to see him. I'm not sure why I want to see Finn, or if I'm even going to speak with him, but my feet are taking me to him all the same. I need some kind of closure for a relationship that never existed. Because even while I've dated other guys, Finn was always there, in the back of my mind, as this idealized forever guy. For most of my life I've planned on Finn. So sure. Confident in my direction. Until this week. This uncertain girl stuff is not me, and I'm over it. I'm letting go of this *idea* I have of Finn. Because Sawyer is real.

The door to Finn's office is open and the light is on when I get to his corridor of the building. For once, by luck, not because I've strategized bumping into him. He's alone, and he beams when he sees me. Positively lights up. Which is weird. It makes me feel nothing but curiosity, which is I guess what I came here to confirm. That my childish crush has indeed ended like a ripped-off Band-Aid. Quick and efficient, with just a small bite of pain.

"Everly!" Finn is out of his chair and around his desk hugging me before I know what's hit me. What? I'm not familiar with unsolicited bursts of affection from Finn. Not even solicited ones, come to think of it.

"Hey, Finn," I murmur in return as he lets me go and steps back, then perches on the end of his desk, his hands wrapped around the edge, a smile still on his face.

"You and Sawyer," he says.

Me and Sawyer what?

"I'd never have expected the two of you," he continues, shaking his head a little and looking as pleased as I've ever seen him. "But you're exactly what he needs."

"What?" Seriously, what?

"I think you're the only girl on earth who could have wrangled him so quickly," he continues with a laugh. "Wow,

Everly Jensen and my brother. Eric's gonna be pissed."

What in the hell is he talking about? My phone vibrates in my pocket, reminding me that it's been on silent for a few hours. There was a test in my last class, all cells and laptops off, so I've been offline since lunch. The phone vibrates again and I slip it out of my pocket to see it lit up with notifications.

"Anyway," Finn continues, and I realized I've missed whatever he was saying. What was he insinuating about Sawyer and I? Did Sawyer tell him he's pursuing me? I guess that makes sense. Finn clearly told Sawyer about my unrequited crush and ensuing shenanigans, of course Sawyer would tell his brother.

"Did you stop by for something?" Finn asks, pushing himself off the desk and checking his watch. "I've got a class in ten minutes."

"No, I didn't need anything. I was just in the area and wanted to say hi." I pause. "And apologize." I stop and take a breath. "For being a general pain in your ass."

He just nods in response as he slings an arm around my shoulder and walks me to the door. "You've always been unpredictably entertaining," he deadpans.

I laugh as I leave his office and head back outside. I make it to the end of the hall before my phone vibrates again and I remember all the notifications. I make it a few more steps before I have to stop walking and focus on my phone, because what I'm seeing isn't making sense. A voicemail from Eric and a corresponding text simply stating, *CALL ME.* A missed call from Sophie and a text stating, *Confused?* And from Chloe, a Facebook message—*Players gonna play, schemers gonna scheme*—followed by a bunch of emoticons that are smiling so hard they're crying.

I hit the notification tab and scroll back a few hours. All the usual. Likes, comments, friend requests. Wait. Most of the likes and comments seem to be on... my relationship status? I never use that feature. Like, ever. I click on one of the notifications, taking me to the post.

Everly Jensen is in a relationship with Sawyer Camden.

Hold on. Hold. The fuck. On.

I'm not even friends with him. I'd know. I'm not one of those girls who just adds anyone. I always look first, and I have most definitely not added him.

Except it appears that I did. The update on my wall prior to my newfound relationship status is:

Everly Jensen and Sawyer Camden are friends.

The time stamp: two hours ago. Two hours ago, when I was in class, with no internet.

That son of a bitch hacked me.

Twenty-Two

"Who does that?" I'm fuming. "Who breaks into someone's Facebook account and updates their relationship status?"

I'm on the phone with Chloe. My tirade is met with silence, then tears. You know, the kind of tears you get when you're laughing so hard you cry? Those. She gasps for breath while I wait.

"Chloe, this is serious."

"You're right, you're right." She blows out a breath while trying to compose herself. "Seriously"—she clears her throat—"it is pretty bad. Not, say, physical breaking and entering bad, but close, right?"

I gasp. "Oh, nooooo, you did not just say that!"

"I did!" She's back to laughing and I hear a thump. I'm pretty sure she just laughed herself off her bed. I've reached the front doors of Hymer and I push through them, anxious to keep moving, even though I've no idea where my destination is. "It's not as bad as, say, making a fake dating profile for your friend and sending them on a date without telling them," she deadpans, then breaks into a fit of giggles.

I'm never gonna live that one down, so I roll my eyes even though she's not there to see it and then jog down the steps outside the building.

"I've got to go, Chloe, I'll call you later." I shouldn't have called her. It was a total violation of the first rule of proper complaining. Pick the right audience for your complaint.

"Sawyer Camden is officially my new favorite person! I

hope you're very happy together!" she says in a singsong before I can hang up.

I reach the bottom step and stop. I pull my jacket closed and think. I really don't have any idea where I'm going. I need to talk to that arrogant asshole, obviously. And that's when I realize I have no idea how to contact him. He's not left his phone number on any of the cards that were sent. I don't know where he lives, other than somewhere in the Philadelphia area, and the one person who could tell me, Finn, just went to teach a class.

I groan. So that's what Finn was going on about. He must have seen the Facebook update about Sawyer and I. Shit, my mom is going to see that Facebook status and ask me a hundred questions that I have none of the answers to. She's probably adding Sawyer to her Christmas list right now.

Couldn't he have just called me? Like a normal person?

I should Google him. I can't believe I haven't done it already. I am so off my game. Wait, I can use Facebook. Might as well, since he went through all the trouble of hacking my account to accept his own friend request. I tap open the app on my phone and pull up his profile. I could message him this way, or... let's see what we have to work with here.

Works at Clemens Corp.

Of course he does. Clemens Corp is a technology company. They just made headlines for selling a multi-billion-dollar web browsing project to the entertainment industry. They've also developed apps you likely use every day. GPS apps for tracking your children or spouse, that kind of thing. It's the hot place to work in Philadelphia. The perks are supposedly amazing, like using technology before it's released, free on-site daycare, a free cafeteria, that kind of thing. He probably used company time and resources to break into my account. *Real appropriate, Sawyer.*

But the good news is their headquarters are in Logan Square, and I know exactly where the building is.

I Uber myself a ride and say a silent prayer of thanks when the app tells me a car will be here in three minutes. I could walk to Logan Square, it's less than two miles, but I'm in a hurry. Plus, let's be real. I want to look good when I arrive, so I'm not hiking over there.

My Uber ride arrives and we shoot over to Market Street. The driver agrees with me, by the way, about Sawyer being completely out of line with this Facebook stunt. See, know your audience. It helps that he has none of the backstory, and I'm the customer so he's probably going to agree with me anyway, but still. It's much more satisfying than venting to Chloe.

We loop around City Hall Station then past JFK Plaza before hitting traffic on the Benjamin Franklin Parkway. I check my Facebook app and fume some more.

The car finally pulls up to Logan Square and I thank my new friend Tom and hop out, then head straight for the revolving doors. Once I've whooshed through them I realize I've got two problems. One, there's security, and I can't just grab an elevator. And two, I have no idea where to find him in this fifty-story building. Well, no matter.

My phone dings. It's my mom, asking if Sawyer eats red meat because she's thinking of making a roast for Christmas. I think my nostrils actually flare as I march up to the security desk and slap my hands on the counter.

"I need to see Sawyer Camden. Now."

The smile drops from the guard's face and a bored look replaces it. "Ma'am, we don't have an on-site customer service department. If you go to our website there's a 'contact us' tab at the top of the page. You can't miss it." He gives me an uninterested smile. "Or I can give you a card with our 1-800 number," he says, placing one on the countertop when I don't move.

"I don't need customer service, I need to see Sawyer Camden. He works here, and I'd like to see him." I smile tightly, trying not to take out my frustration with Sawyer on the poor guy at the desk. I wave at the phone behind the counter. "Call him or give me a guest pass or something."

The guard doesn't make any moves to pick up the phone,

but he does tilt his head and observe me a little closer, as if I'm being irrational and might need to be dealt with.

"Ma'am, I'm going to have to ask you to—"

"Everly!"

The guard and I both snap our gazes up. A blonde woman clicks across the lobby to reach us. "Everly Jensen?" she asks, but more as a courtesy than because she's unsure.

"Yes," I agree, cautiously. She clearly belongs here, the guard murmuring a "Miss Adams," and tipping his head to her upon her arrival. She's wearing the cutest black jacket over a skirt, paired with a pair of heels I'm coveting. Her blonde hair is pulled into a low pony, the ends of it curled in what looks like a natural wave. An official building ID badge clipped to her waist completes the outfit.

She beams and holds out a hand. "I'm Sandra, Mr. Camden's assistant," she says. "I wasn't expecting you or I'd have made sure you had building clearance. I'm so sorry," she adds, and it's totally genuine. "Ted," she addresses the guard, "I'll take her up with me and send you a clearance to be held on file for her at the desk."

He nods with a, "Ma'am," even though he's old enough to be this woman's father, and with that we're through the turnstiles and she's swiping her badge at the elevators.

"He's in a meeting. I'll bring you up and let him know you're here, but I'm not sure if he can step out this second," she adds, and she says it apologetically, as if I'm the one who's being inconvenienced.

We've just stepped into an empty elevator car and I'm rapidly questioning my decision to crash his workplace unannounced. He deserves it after the stunt he pulled today, but this is too weird, even for me. "You know, I could come back at a better time," I offer as the elevator slows to a stop.

"No, no." Her eyes widen in alarm at the suggestion that I should leave. "It's no trouble at all, promise. I can't imagine he'd be pleased if you left without saying hello," she adds, another smile on her face.

Uh. Okay. I can't imagine he's gonna be pleased when I

give him a piece of my mind, but hell, I'm already here.

The doors slide open and a man around Sawyer's age steps on. He's in jeans and a button-down shirt, the sleeves rolled back and shoved up to the elbow, a stark contrast to Sandra's attire. Probably a tech nerd. They always get away with casual attire in the workplace. Hot though. He's wearing chunky nerd glasses that frame his face perfectly. Well, at least now I don't feel so out of place in my distressed jeans tucked into a pair of boots. No, not *the* boots. Not that I sent them back, but I haven't worn them. Besides, it's supposed to snow today, which sadly requires Lands' End, not Louboutin.

"Sandra," the man greets her and gives me a little nod.

"Mr. Laurent," she returns, but her voice sounds different than it did a moment ago. Reverent. Maybe the guy's important. But there's something more, I suspect. I eye her and watch as her gaze drops to his ass when he reaches out to punch a floor on the control panel. Oh! She is totally into the hot tech nerd! I wonder if I can help. I do love helping.

The doors slide closed and the elevator is again ascending, this time into a cloud of awkward silence. They really do need my help.

"Sandra, I love your shoes," I say, glancing down. But I'm not looking at her shoes. I tilt my head as if I am, but it's just a ruse so I can see if this Mr. Laurent takes the opportunity to check out her legs while we're both distracted looking at her shoes.

He does. Which most any guy would—she's got fabulous legs. But his gaze lingers a moment longer than necessary and then he swallows and clears his throat. It's subtle. No way Sandra is catching this, but I am. I verify that he is ring free and then, satisfied, I tuck the information away until I can use it. This day is really turning around.

Twenty-Three

The elevator stops and we exit, Mr. Laurent doing that thing men do, holding the elevator door open for us as if it's capable of squashing us to death if not for them holding back the doors. It's nice, plus I'm sure it gives him the opportunity to check out Sandra's ass. Win, win.

"Is Sawyer still in the Chesterfield meeting?" Mr. Laurent pauses outside the elevator, directing the question to Sandra.

"Yes, sir. They're in the Langhorne conference room."

The corner of his mouth arcs in the smallest smirk at her use of the word 'sir.' "You've worked here for two years, Sandra. I believe I've mentioned you can call me Gabe?"

Her eyes widen and she nods, but when she speaks it's with fake confidence. "Of course!" And then with the smallest lift of her head, she says, "Gabe."

He looks at her a second longer, then nods and heads in the opposite direction from us.

Sandra guides me to the right, down a wide hallway and past a glass-walled conference room before I can't contain myself any longer.

"Two years?" We're walking at a very efficient pace down the hall, Sandra's ponytail swishing with each step.

Her steps don't falter but her head turns in my direction and she asks, "Pardon?"

"That"—I point to her and then point in the direction that Gabe disappeared in—"has been going on for two years?" I'm incredulous. There is no way that has been simmering for two years, unfulfilled.

She blinks rapidly and opens her mouth to speak, then closes it. "I'm sorry?" she tries, clearly out of her element in how to respond to an Everly-style inquisition. The hallway ends at a corner, with another wide hallway leading across the building, but we stop here and step into a foyer of sorts. There's a desk—I'm assuming it's hers based on a quick glance around. A sweater hangs over the back of the chair and a pink notepad sits on the desk. Two chairs are placed across from the desk and a small couch stands along the wall near a set of open double doors that I assume lead to Sawyer's office. Pretty fancy stuff.

"May I take your jacket?" she asks, and I slip it off and hand it to her and pull down the sleeves of my sweater to the tops of my fingers. Sandra hangs my coat in a closet near the door, and then offers me a seat.

"You can wait here," she says, turning back to me. She offers to get me a drink, I insist I don't need anything and then she's off, promising to let Sawyer know I'm here but reiterating that he is in a meeting so please be patient.

The second she's gone I stand and enter the attached office. Floor-to-ceiling windows line the entire office space. I step right up to the edge and place my forehead against the glass. Holy shit, the view from up here is insane. We must be on the top floor. Logan Square looks bigger than you'd think from up here. The fountain surrounded by grass is easy to make out. The cars rounding the circular drive are tiny though. Turning around, I survey the room. It's probably four times the size of my dorm room, maybe more. There's a large desk with two chairs in front of it and a separate seating area with a sofa and chairs by the wall with the refrigerator that is hidden behind decorative paneling.

There's a kitchenette section lining the wall adjoining the outer office. I check out the contents of the fridge. Not because I want anything, just 'cause I'm nosey. But he has Diet Sun Drop and I love Diet Sun Drop. I love it almost as much as I love new shoes, so I grab a can and move on to the desk. I hesitate for a moment. This can't be Sawyer's office, can it? It's really impressive. But Sandra's desk is just outside. This must be his office. I chew on my lip for a moment then plop in the chair behind the desk. There's a desktop computer, but it's locked, obviously. Which is fine, because even though Sawyer hacked my Facebook, physical snooping is more my thing.

There's not much on the surface of the desk. A pen, a couple of Post-Its. It's very disappointing. But then everything is digital nowadays, so anything entertaining is probably on his computer. I set my soda on the desk and open the drawer. It's weird the way security didn't want to let me in the building. Nothing in the drawers either. How annoying.

"Find anything interesting?"

It's Sawyer.

Of course.

Twenty-Four

"No." I slide the drawer shut and, standing, glare at him. I push my hair over my shoulders and get ready to lay into him. "What is wrong with you? You hacked my Facebook, Sawyer! That is not okay. My mother is messaging me wanting to know what you like to eat for Christmas dinner," I hiss. "I am going to kill you."

He grins and closes the office door behind him, the click loud enough for me to hear across the room.

"Look, weirdo. I don't know how you normally conduct your relationships, but what you did? Not okay."

"I needed to get your attention. I'd say it worked."

"My attention?" My eyebrows shoot up in disbelief. "Try a phone next time, Sawyer."

He shrugs and walks towards me. "You never gave me your phone number."

I pinch the bridge of my nose and groan. "Hacking my Facebook to accept your friend request and publicly declaring that we're dating was easier than getting my phone number?"

"I can't say it was hard."

I exhale and shake my head. "Is this your office?" I glance around the room again, a little dubious.

"It is." He's standing in front of me now, across the desk. He stops and places his hands in his pockets. He's wearing a suit. Wearing the hell out of the suit, actually. I run my gaze down his body. I don't try to hide it, because why? There's no point with this guy. Clearly I can be myself and whatever I throw at him, he's just going to laugh.

"Are you somebody important here?" I ask, gesturing to the building in general.

"Does it matter? All I want to be is somebody to you." He says it sincerely, his eyes on mine, his gaze not wavering.

"Your brother is really excited for us, Sawyer," I say softly, my fight gone. "He thinks I've tamed you or some nonsense. Do you need taming?"

"Miss Beverly Cleary Jensen," he starts, but I interrupt immediately.

"Oh, God. You went that deep? What'd you do, pull my birth certificate? No one calls me Beverly."

"Your passport. I wanted to make sure you had one."

"Sure." I nod. "Totally normal." I glance around the room again and cross my arms across my chest. I wonder how big a player he is. Swanky office. Attractive as hell. His own brother's comments, not to mention my brother warning him to stay away from me last weekend. I bet he's had sex in here, I think, eyeing him again.

"Yes, I've had sex in my office," he says, answering my unasked question. "I wasn't going to suggest it for our first time together as I'm not sure how loud you are." He pauses, gesturing outside his office. "Lots of people working out there, but we can give it a try if you want."

I snort. So fucking confident, this guy. "I bet. I bet women bend right over this desk for you," I lean forward and place my hands on the desk and drop one shoulder seductively. "I bet they're all, 'Oh, Sawyer, it's so big. I don't think it's gonna fit.' Newsflash for you. They're lying. It always fits."

He's silent, watching my little show. Then a slow smile spreads across his face, his eyes amused. "I really like you."

What? I just insulted his dick and he's complimenting me. I eye him, wary.

He rounds the desk and I turn as he does so and now we're toe to toe. He's much taller than I am so I'm forced to look up, or stare at his chest. The button of his shirt is less than a foot from me, and I'm oddly tempted to run my fingers over it, but I keep my hands to myself and tilt my neck back. I take my time though, running my tongue over my lips and taking in his jaw on my way to meeting his eyes. I have a thing for a good jaw line on a man. I could spend hours on a good jaw, starting with a nip to an earlobe and working my way down. His skin fascinates me, the hint of a five-o'clock shadow present, the texture, that jaw-clench thing. Is there a term for that?

By the time my eyes reach his they're hooded. He wraps the fingers of one hand behind my neck, his thumb under my jaw, and then his lips are on mine. I'm expecting it this time, unlike outside my dorm, but it doesn't change the current that runs through me with his touch. I move my hands to his chest, inside his jacket, and he's warm under my palms, my hands sliding greedily over his shirt, desperate to feel the ridges of his chest.

My ass is on his desk and my legs are wrapped around his waist when he tears himself away from me. It takes me a second to catch up, unsure for a moment how I even got onto his desk. He steps back and clears his throat, straightening his jacket, and it's the hottest thing I've ever seen a man do, but I want him to take it off, not straighten it out. He's adjusting the cuffs of his shirt, then his tie as I come back to reality and realize how out of control that got very quickly. The adjustment of his pants confirms that. And hell, I can already see that despite my earlier teasing, he probably has heard the words, *It's not gonna fit.*

I straighten on the desk and he offers me his hand, helping me slide off to my feet.

"I'll pick you up at seven," he murmurs, his lips close to my ear, the heat of his breath causing a shiver to run through me.

I nod, because really, I was never not going to agree to this. I didn't stand a chance.

"I'm not sleeping with you tonight, just so you know." He brushes a stray strand of hair off my face and tucks it behind my ear.

Excuse me?

"I need you to respect me first," he continues, his eyes somber.

"You cannot be serious," I blurt out a moment before he starts to laugh.

He winks at me and pinches my ass, letting me know he's teasing. Thank fuck. I'm so turned on from that make-out session on his desk. I haven't had sex in a few months. I wasn't dating anyone during my 'make Finn fall in love with me' campaign this fall, which is probably why I've been behaving like such a nut job.

Sandra is outside the office, leaning against the edge of her desk, looking like she's ready to start biting her nails from nerves when Sawyer opens the door to his office. She straightens, concern crossing her face. "Mr. Camden, they're quite anxious to wrap up the meeting..." She trails off as the phone on her desk rings. Her eyes dart to the phone and back to Sawyer.

She is way too young to be so wound up.

"Tell them I'm on my way," he says, not seeming the least bit bothered that people are waiting on him. He rests his hand low on my back and guides me through the door. His hand is large and firm on my back, the heat of his skin pressing through my sweater, and I want to push him back into the office and tell Sandra to hold all his calls. But Sawyer has already murmured, "Tonight," in my ear and disappeared down the hallway. Damn, can he wear a suit.

"They can't even finish the meeting without him, huh?" I say to Sandra once she finishes with her phone call. I flash her a grin and roll my eyes in jest.

She looks startled by my joke, then shakes her head. "Well, no, not really. He doesn't attend every single meeting, obviously." She smiles, but I'm starting to remember something Chloe said—

"Oh! I almost forgot." Sandra pulls open a drawer in her desk and slides something out of a tray inside. It clangs like coins do when you drag them across a desk top and scoop them into your hand, but what she holds up is not pocket change. It's a shiny silver keychain, with keys dangling. Sandra reaches them out to me, dropping the key ring in my palm.

"What are these?" I ask her, holding the keys up for closer inspection. They're identical. Three of them.

Her expression falters a bit, her brow wrinkling in concern. "Sawyer's keys. Well, his key, really. He asked me to give them to you. It's all the same key. He said you'd need three," she adds, as if it's that last detail that threw her.

I want to throw back my head and laugh, but she has no idea I don't even know where he lives, I realize. She obviously thinks I'm his girlfriend. I mean, I guess everyone does, since he announced it on Facebook. But she thinks it's real. Like I've been to his place and left shampoo in his shower. Like I know when his birthday is. Not like we're going on our first date tonight.

Sandra says goodbye to me at the elevators, waving with a friendly smile as if she's just made a new friend, and I step into the car alone, my mind whirling.

Chloe had commented on their names, Sawyer and Finn. "Parents had a Mark Twain thing going on, huh?" she'd said. Mark Twain, which, if I'm remembering my high-school reading assignments correctly, was a pen name. A quick look on the internet via my cell phone confirms it. Mark Twains' real name was Samuel Langhorne Clemens.

The elevator opens at the lobby and I step out, phone still in my hand, and make my way to the lobby entrance. CLEMENS CORP is attached to the wall in glossy three-foot letters over the security desk, matching the giant sign attached to the top of this building, and all the pieces fall into place.

This is Sawyer's building.

Twenty-Five

"I cannot believe I didn't Google him this week." I'm at my desk typing away while Chloe grins at me from across the room. I've showered and shaved my legs, moisturized everywhere with a sugar-lemon body lotion, and blow-dried my hair. Now I'm stewing.

"Why didn't I Google him?" I'm incredulous. I am the queen of invasiveness. I Googled Sophie's boyfriend before she did. I set up an internet dating profile for Chloe without her knowledge *and* sent her on a date. Yet I was so distracted I didn't even think of Googling Sawyer once this week. I'm slipping. I'm twenty-two years old and I'm already losing my touch.

"On the plus side, it probably made barging into his office today easier, not knowing who he was," Chloe says, trying not to laugh, so it turns into a snort.

"No wonder the security guard thought I was an idiot," I grumble, dropping my chin into my hand. "They tried to direct me to customer service, Chloe." I'm mulling over my embarrassment when an even worse thought occurs to me. "He probably has sex with supermodels," I say, my eyes widening.

"So what? Isn't there a saying about that? Show me a supermodel and I'll show you a guy who's tired of fucking her?" Chloe asks, flopping onto her bed. "Something like that?"

"Um, I think so. But how is that helpful? Wouldn't he just

move onto the next supermodel?"

She thinks for a second. "Well, nobody ever said supermodels were great in bed or anything."

I sit up and shoot her a look that says, *Nice try*. "But they're so tall," I say, standing and moving to the mirror, eyeing myself. "He's almost a foot taller than me."

"Supermodels are bony."

I chew on my lip and think. "Yeah, that's valid." I am pretty curvy for being so tiny. I check out my butt in the mirror. "What am I going to wear?" I ask, scanning the clock as I sit back down and pull up my Pinterest account. Typing *date with billionaire* into the search engine does not pull up anything useful. Humph.

"Did he say where you're going?"

"No. He just said he'd pick me up at seven. And I left there without his phone number."

"You could always call Finn and ask him for it," Chloe suggests impishly while tearing open a package of Animal Crackers, immediately dunking one into a tub of Nutella.

I wrinkle my nose. "Ugh. That stuff is disgusting."

"You don't know what you're missing," she retorts and pops another one in her mouth.

"I think I do. I've tasted it. And it's nasty," I tell her as my phone chirps. It's a text. From Sawyer.

Dress warm. Casual. Jeans are good.

"Son of a bitch. He does have my number."

Chloe claps her hands and grins. "This is better than movie night!" she squeals, then holds up the Nutella. "I should put this away and pop some popcorn."

I thought you said you didn't have my number.

Let's see what he has to say about that.

I said you never gave it to me, not that I didn't have it.

Aren't you clever.

And wear the boots I sent. They'll look good later wrapped around my neck.

I don't respond to that.

"Chloe, is it slutty that I kinda want to skip this date and go straight back to his place for sex?"

"Do you care if it's slutty?"

"Just on principle."

She pops another Nutella-covered Animal Cracker in her mouth while she thinks, holding up a finger to indicate she's gonna give this some serious thought. I pull out my nail polish and survey my options. Aha! Perfect. It's red and its name is Size Matters. How can I get a job naming nail polish colors? I'd be so good at it. I mean, I really understand the importance of the right polish name. It absolutely sets the mood of an entire outfit.

"It's a little bit slutty." Chloe's finished chewing and has given me her verdict. "You really should buy him dinner first."

I nod. "That's fair." I pull on my favorite jeans and then survey my choices before pulling on a sweater over a lacy camisole. He said casual. This one is the perfect chocolate brown and makes my eyes pop, and the lace camisole peeps out of the bottom. Perfect. The weather is nice for early December and the snow that was threatening earlier today never materialized. I've got a cute camel-colored pea coat that will complement the sweater, in case I want to leave it unbuttoned. Finally, I pull out the Louboutin box from under the bed. He did specify that I should wear them after all, and I'm a very accommodating girl. Most of the time. Hardly ever.

I use a fat curling iron to add a few big waves to my hair and then complete my makeup with smoky eyes and dark, chocolatey-red lipstick. He's definitely going to want to skip dinner when he sees me, I decide, looking myself over before I head out.

At five to seven I tell Chloe I'm going down to the lobby to wait for him and she groans.

"He's not coming upstairs? I was gonna take pictures," she jokes, holding up her phone. "Maybe I'll just come down with you and grab a few before you go." She pretends like she's getting off the bed, making a big production out of it.

"Zip it, roomie. I'll see you later."

"By later, you mean tomorrow?"

"I sure as hell hope so."

Twenty-Six

Sawyer is waiting for me when I get downstairs. He's leaning against the wall with the mailboxes, hands in his pockets, posture relaxed while he surveys the hustle and bustle in the lobby. Based on his expression I'd say he's amused. There are a couple of guys lounging on the sofas, tossing a basketball between them. Two different pizza delivery drivers waiting for students to meet them in the lobby to collect their orders. A couple having an argument near the elevators. And at least four girls who are eyeing the fuck out of him.

I see him before he sees me. I use the time to take him in. He's painfully good-looking. He's changed since I saw him this afternoon. The suit is gone, replaced with faded denim jeans and a grey v-neck sweater, the collar of a white button-down shirt appearing underneath. His dark hair is tousled, as if he showered after work and just ran his hands through it while it dried. I cannot wait to get my hands on that hair. I know it must be as thick as it looks, and I'm a bit fascinated with the barely-there wave. It'll definitely be something to hold on to later.

He sees me coming and his eyes do a slow trail down my frame and then back again. "You pick up all your dates here?" I quip.

He exhales slowly and shakes his head. "I didn't think there was a woman alive who could have me waiting on her in a college dorm," he replies. "But then again, I wasn't expecting you, Boots."

Well, hell, I don't have a reply for that. I stare in his eyes for a moment and nod, the moment strangely intimate. He has the most devastating blue eyes, and I'm finding I really like having their attention on me.

He helps me into my coat and we head out. As he holds the car door for me I realize I still don't know where we're going, and it's nice. Not planning the date is fan-freaking-tastic. I don't have to think about it. I don't have to ask him what he wants to do and worry about him having a good time. I just get to have fun. Sawyer might be right about being pursued versus doing the pursuing. Unless he's about to take me to a strip club.

We make it as far as 5th Street, which isn't far at all, when I remember that I Googled him today. And that I know too much. Like his middle name (Thomas) and his birthday (January twenty-seventh) and his net worth (a lot). All stuff I should not yet know. It's probably no more information than he's dug up on me, but still, it feels weird. It might be the billions part that makes it weird. It's definitely the billions part.

I fidget in my seat and then ask if he had a good day at work.

"The afternoon was pretty tedious. I had to sit through a meeting with a raging hard-on."

"Sorry," I mumble. I don't even mumble it sarcastically.

"What's going on here, Boots? No snappy retort from you?" We're stopped at a light by the hospital. An ambulance whizzes past, the red and blue lights slicing through the car.

"Nothing is going on." I shake my head and sit up straighter.

"Ah, you finally Googled me, didn't you?" he says, smirking.

"Um, yeah."

"Don't do that. Don't act differently."

"Is that why you like me? No one else will call you an asshole to your face?"

"It's a struggle, Boots, a real struggle to find that kind of honesty. I cry into my thousand-thread-count custom-made

Kleenex all the time. Sure, I can get Siri to call me an asshole, but it's hard to take a phone seriously, you know? She lacks the acrimony."

"Siri does no such thing," I respond, but I'm smiling.

"I do not lie, Everly Jensen. Do it right now."

I'm laughing now, but I'm game. I swipe my phone and hit the home button, summoning the Siri feature, and request that she call me an asshole. When she responds in her pleasant robot voice, requesting confirmation that from now on she'll call me "Asshole," we both completely lose it.

I'm still calming myself from my giggle fit when we pull into a parking garage. I see a logo for the Ritz-Carlton as we glide past it. Seriously? Okay, yes, I was sorta hoping we could skip to this part, but a hotel? Billionaires are all the same. I've only met one, but they're probably all the same. Arrogant. And weird. A hotel? His house would have been fine.

"I cannot believe you brought me to a hotel." I gasp. "Is this your version of Netflix and chill? It's not cool, Sawyer. Not cool." I'm getting really into it now, waving my arms around. "A hotel? Are you one of those weird billionaires who can't even take a woman to their house? You said we were going on a date." I finish in a huff, dropping my hands in my lap.

Your move, Sawyer.

He pulls into a parking spot and kills the engine before turning to me and resting his arm over the back of my headrest. He leans in and meets my gaze head on, pausing for a second before responding.

"I live here," he says, completely straight-faced. "Not in the hotel, that would be"—he pauses, recalling my wording—"weirdly billionaire of me. I live in the residential tower. In a condo, not a hotel room."

Oh.

"Also, I'm just parking the car. We're going to Love Park. It's a couple blocks"—he points over my shoulder—"that way."

Well, shit. I'm tapping a finger on my chin trying to think a way out of this fake tantrum when he can't keep a straight face anymore and grins.

"You are the worst actress, Everly."

"Am not!" I cannot believe he just said that to me. My drama is on point.

"Are so."

"Trust me, you would not believe the stuff I get away with," I boast. Wait. I probably shouldn't have said that out loud. I frown and bite my lip.

"I don't doubt it, Boots. You've been a constant source of entertainment in my life, that's for sure. Yet now that I've met you, I can't get enough of you."

"You don't think I'm a bit much?" I hold my breath. Everyone thinks I'm a bit much.

"Never."

Twenty-Seven

We exit the parking garage and he takes my hand like he's been holding it my whole life, and it's nice. I'm not sure where we're going, but as soon as we round the corner from Penn Square to 15th Street I see the lights from Love Park straight ahead.

"You're taking me to the Christmas Village?" I can feel the grin spreading across my face. Every December there's an outdoor market reminiscent of the traditional Christmas Villages popular all across Germany. I've heard about it, but in my three and a half years living in Philadelphia I've never gone.

"I thought we could walk around a bit and then get dinner."

It's perfect. The weather is cooperating tonight, and it's just cold enough to make it feel festive without being miserable. The park is lined with wooden booths, featuring an assortment of crafts, pottery, jewelry, toys, almost anything you could think of. And food. Pretzels, strudel, gingerbread, crepes, stollen, bratwurst, chocolates and Belgian waffles. Round that off with a couple of wine booths and a hot chocolate stand and what you have is pure joy.

We walk the booths lining the perimeter of the fountain, currently replaced with a giant Christmas tree that must be two stories tall. It's packed with people, and we dodge other patrons with my hand still firmly in Sawyer's. At one booth we find dog treats for his parents' dog, whose name is Sam, by the way. We compare notes on growing up with mothers so obsessed with reading that they name their children and pets after literary characters or authors. About how much it annoyed me as a first grader to be saddled with an old-fashioned name like Beverly, so I dropped the B and insisted everyone call me Everly until it stuck. But that secretly, I loved every single book ever written by Beverly Cleary and still have each paperback stashed in the attic hideaway above my childhood bedroom.

We try Glühwein, a spiced mulled wine which I love and Sawyer wants no part of, and stollen, which I assume will be dry like a biscotti but turns out to be closer to a heavy cake—and delicious. We laugh when we stumble upon Christmas ornaments made from old library cards and immediately buy them for both of our mothers.

The atmosphere is undeniably romantic, the city lights a backdrop to this little slice of the North Pole, popped into a city park as if by magic.

I spot a tent selling bratwursts and drag Sawyer over.

"When I said dinner I meant a reservation at Del Frisco's," he says, looking a little bewildered by my request.

I shake my head. "Can you cancel it? I want to stay here and eat brats standing up in a crowd of people," I plead.

He agrees, and I order two brats, mustard only for both of us. He steps back with his hands up when I elbow in front of him to pay.

"Sorry, I had to buy you dinner," I explain while I unwrap half of my brat, like a burrito.

"Why's that?" he asks, taking a bite of his.

"My roommate insisted it's the polite thing to do before I fuck you." I say it just loud enough for him to hear. He clears his throat, mid chew, then swallows before speaking. A slow, sexy grin follows before he speaks.

"Will you call me in the morning?" His eyes flicker with amusement.

"No." I shake my head slowly. "I won't have left yet, as I'll be expecting you to make me breakfast after I bought you this expensive dinner"—I signal the brats—"and made you come."

He nods, and suddenly the mood changes from

lighthearted to intense. His gaze on my face is all-consuming and the crowd of people and lights and noise is reduced to a dull buzz on the periphery of my mind. I like the way he looks at me, like he gets me. Like he wants more of me. Like I interest him.

He slides a hand around my lower back and bends closer. His breath brushes my ear and it sends a shiver through me. "I'd be happy to," he murmurs and then brushes one kiss on the skin behind my ear.

I'm wet. Like I'm gonna have to ditch these panties before he sees them wet. From a simple kiss. He didn't even say anything dirty, but my heart is racing.

I want him. Right now. And the fact that we're outdoors in a public park is slowly coming back to me. I'm doubtful I can convince him to have his way with me behind Santa's workshop surrounded by a crowd of people, so I better pull myself together.

We finish our brats and walk the booths aligning JFK Boulevard, grabbing hot chocolate at one as the temperature starts to dip. I wrap my hands around the paper cup, watching the steam rise off and dissipate in the cold air. I scrunch my shoulders to ward off the chill and take a sip.

"You're cold. We should head out."

Yes! Yes, yes, all the yeses.

I play it cool and simply nod in agreement, turning to the direction we came in from. It's a short walk, and in minutes we're inside the lobby of the Ritz-Carlton. A moment later, before I know what's hit me, we're being seated. In the lounge. For drinks. Why? Why are we having drinks? This is not where I thought we were headed. I thought we were on the same page, the sex page. A really hot, dirty sex page that's earmarked so you can read it again and again.

I have to actively stop myself from sighing as I take a seat. It's nice in here, pretty swanky. We're seated around a small round cocktail table in matching leather club chairs. The kind of chair you can comfortably cross your legs in, which, no, that's not helping. I clench all the spots that so desperately want attention right now and bounce my foot.

A waiter arrives, placing bar napkins on the table top and asking what we'd like. Sawyer tilts his head in my direction, indicating I should order.

"I'd like a screwdriver," I say, looking at Sawyer, not the waiter.

His lip curves upward in amusement before he turns his attention back to the waiter and orders himself a whiskey, neat. The waiter leaves and Sawyer rubs his chin, his elbow resting on the arm of the chair, his amused eyes on my miffed ones.

Then we talk. We talk and I've got to admit it's nice, sitting here with him, even though I know this little pit stop was just designed to make me crazy. He's not checked his cell phone once tonight, I realize, and neither have I. I'm not sure I've ever been on a date that didn't involve a cell phone before.

Our drinks arrive and we both take a sip, Sawyer inquiring if the drink is to my liking. It is. He is. I like spending time with him. He's easy to be with—it's easy to be myself with him. He's attentive, and I'm interested in everything he has to say. The chemistry, this pull I feel towards him, I can't put into words. It's almost too good to be true. And that therein is my fear. What if we're sexually incompatible? It happens.

I take another sip of my drink and contemplate downing it in one gulp. But no. That'd get me tipsy and I'm pretty sure Sawyer will not put out if I'm anything close to drunk. I tap my finger against the side of the glass and estimate that it's going to take at least twenty minutes for us to finish these drinks. Then a worse thought occurs to me. What if he orders another round and we're stuck in here for an hour or longer? I wrinkle my nose and set the glass down on the table, then lean in closer to Sawyer, my fingers stroking the arm of the chair, and drop my voice.

"It's so loud in here. Maybe we should go someplace quieter," I suggest. But I realize too late, as it's coming out of my mouth, that it's not too loud in here. In fact, I'd describe the sound level as distinctly subdued. Damn it, I can't take it back, I already said it. Maybe he hasn't noticed how quiet it is, so I add, "Don't you think?" in a whisper.

He has to bite his lip to keep from laughing. I'm watching him—he's physically rolled his lip inward to restrain himself.

"Everly?" He leans in closer, his voice soft, seductive.

"Yes?"

"Did you want to be done talking now?"

I nod, relieved. "Yes." I sit up a little straighter, ready to grab my bag and hoof it out of here. He relaxes, sitting back in his chair. I stifle a groan.

"You're awfully anxious to get in my pants, Boots."

I slump back into the very comfortable chair and cross my arms, shrugging. "You might be terrible in bed," I admit.

He coughs and that turns into a laugh that he covers with his fist. "Might I?"

I nod, my mood serious. "You might."

"Your seduction techniques are something, Everly."

Oh, my God. He's not denying it. Maybe he has an erectile dysfunction. He's a premature ejaculator. Or he's got a micropenis. Or he's a eunuch. That'd be just my luck, wouldn't it? Wait, I could feel his erection this afternoon in his office. So scratch those last two worries. Still, so many possibilities. I've read articles.

"Do you take any medication?" I blurt out.

He tilts his head and looks at me, "No," he says, then shakes it slowly. "Do you?"

"Just the pill. But you're still wearing a condom. I'm not catching any babies from you." I shudder.

"Assuming I'm able to perform."

"Yes! Exactly!" Finally we're on the same page.

"Yet again, I never know what's going to come out of your mouth."

"I'm an enigma, Sawyer," I say, throwing up my hands, palms up.

He pulls his wallet out and drops cash on the table, then stands, holding his hand out to assist me from my chair.

"Are we going back to your place that is not a hotel room now?"

"We are," he says and continues holding my hand as we walk to the residential tower at the Ritz.

He lets go when he holds the elevator door for me, and then he sticks his hands in his pockets, leaning against the side of the elevator, staring at me.

"What? Why are you staring at me like that?"

"Just deciding what I'm going to do with you first."

"Do with me?" I'm nervous now. I'm not sure I like the sound of that.

He nods, then runs a hand across his jaw, thinking. "Breeding role-play okay?"

"Excuse me?"

"You're cool with video?"

"Look, I have no idea what you're talking about," I say, waving a hand dismissively. "But I'm open to trying whatever your thing is. Unless it's anal. I'm saving anal for marriage."

"Saving anal for marriage," he repeats back to me. "Is that an actual thing?" He's incredulous.

"It's a thing."

"I don't think that's a thing."

"Well, I think it's a thing and it's my ass."

"Fair." He nods. "Just out of curiosity, how do you see that playing out? Wedding night anal? Honeymoon anal? Or are you talking first anniversary anal?"

I twist my lips while I think. "Wedding night anal doesn't seem right, does it?" I scrunch my nose and tap my lip while I give this genuine reflection. "Post-honeymoon, pre-first anniversary seems like the anal sweet spot."

"Good to know. I'll make a note of it."

"You do that."

The elevator stops and we exit. There are two doors on this floor and I follow Sawyer as he unlocks one of them, then pauses on the threshold.

"Do you want me to leave so you can go through my stuff?" He points back to the elevator as if he's serious.

"Cute," I tell him. "Maybe later." Then I step inside and gasp.

Twenty-Eight

Sawyer stops to hang our coats as I take off across the room. Floor-to-ceiling windows line the edge of the condo and the view, I've never seen anything like it. I walk right up to the glass and point.

"Sawyer, William Penn is right there!" I tap the glass with my fingertip. "Like, right there." City Hall is directly across the street with its famed William Penn statue sitting atop the very peak of the clock tower. Being so many floors up, it feels like we're eye level with the statue. I've never seen it from this vantage point, that's for sure. "This is so cool." I'm standing so close to the glass my breath is fogging it up when I speak, so I step back an inch and take in the view. Directly across the street, spotlights highlight the clock tower portion of City Hall. Looking down, I can appreciate the roof of the main building, the architecture stunning from this view. The skyline is sensational, lights twinkling as far as I can see.

I see him approach in the reflection of the glass. I'm still oohing and ahhing over the view when he stops behind me and lays one hand flat on the glass and uses the other to sweep all my hair over my left shoulder, baring the right side of my neck. I watch his reflection in the glass as he bends down and places his lips on the skin where my neck and shoulder meet. My breath hitches instantly, the heat of his lips causing me to go from zero to sixty in a heartbeat. We stand like this for minutes, my chest heaving while he devotes more time than I'd have thought possible to worshiping my neck, his lips traveling up to my ear. I'm wearing dangly earrings, and he slips them out of each lobe, gently, his fingertips skimming my ear as he does, and holy shit, I'm wet again. He's barely touched me, his lips on my neck, his fingertips across my earlobes, yet I'm electrified with need.

His movements are slow. So slow. The man is not in a hurry. His hands move to the hem of my sweater and he raises it, inching it up my torso until he gets to my chest and I raise my arms so he can slide it over my head. I watch the entire show in the reflection of the glass and I want him inside of me so badly that it hurts.

He drops the sweater and winds his hand around a chunk of hair at my scalp, tugging it so softly, as he moves his lips back to my collarbone. I am ready to whimper. And beg. Then he tugs my hair hard and bites my earlobe and I do whimper, my head falling back onto his shoulder.

His hands move to my waist, and I'm sure they're headed for the button of my jeans, but they're not. He slides them up my torso, and I pick my head up to watch in the reflection. My hair is already a mess, my eyelids at half-mast. He's directly behind me, and all I can make out in the reflection are his hands and the top of his head as he moves it to the other side of my neck. He cups my breasts, over my bra, his thumbs rotating simultaneous circles over the lace, moving toward the center with each rotation until he's thumbing my nipples and I'm bending at the waist, trying to grind against him to get some relief, any relief.

The cups of my bra are yanked down, my breasts lewdly resting atop, and then his fingers are back, cupping the weight of them as his thumbs get to work again on my nipples. They're so sensitive right now, his hands so warm and erotic on my skin. I whine and brace my hands on the glass to keep myself upright a moment before he abruptly pinches each nipple and I mewl and drop my elbows to the glass, my head resting on my splayed fingertips.

"Sawyer, please." I've moved on to begging. I want it so bad.

"Please what?" he asks, his palms caressing my tits, the heels of his hands brushing my nipples as he squeezes my flesh between his hands.

"Please take off your pants," I whine.

He doesn't respond, but turns me and slides his hands under my ass until I wrap my legs around his waist. He's still fully clothed, and my nipples rub against his sweater, but it's not where I want the friction. I bury my head in his neck to restrain myself from bouncing in his arms, trying to simulate what I really want to be doing this second.

He carries me like it's nothing to walk with an extra hundred pounds clinging to him and I use the height of my position to finally get my hands into his hair. It's as thick as I thought it would be and I run the pads of my fingers across his scalp, then do a little hair-tugging of my own and run my tongue along the perimeter of his ear.

We come to a stop in his bedroom and he sets me on my feet at the end of his bed. The room is illuminated with the lights from outside the window, the view the same from here as in the main room. Thankfully I'm not shy. He gives me a little shove so I lie back on my elbows, then correctly analyzes that the boots need to come off to pry these jeans off of me and lifts one ankle at a time, making short work of getting them off my feet. My own hands are already on my pants, zipper down, then shimmying them past my butt, lacy bikini bottoms included. Sawyer finishes the job and observes me buck naked on his bed, rubbing his thumb over his bottom lip. He's still dressed. Fucking tease.

"Take. Off. Your pants."

He grins and removes his sweater, then undoes the first few buttons of the button-down he's wearing beneath it, before reaching behind his neck and pulling the shirt off over his head.

"So assertive, Everly."

I lick my lips and ogle his chest. Damn rowers. He is in every bit as good shape as I imagined. My pussy is throbbing, like a physical ache. I want to cross my legs and squeeze, just for the brief pressure it will provide. I consider it, bending my leg and running the toes of one foot up the calf of the opposite leg. But I stop, and bend my knees open instead, exposing myself to him completely. *Come here.*

His shoes make a soft thump on the floor as he toes them off and finally, finally his hands move to his pants, my eyes trailing down the light smattering of hair leading south as he pops the button, unzips, then stops. Why is he stopping?

He drops his forearms to the bed between my spread legs, his intent clear. I slap an open palm on the bedding and mutter, "Goddammit, Sawyer!" as he kisses the spot right above my clit.

He pauses and looks up at me with a smirk, which should be insulting considering where his face is, but I've got more pressing concerns. Namely that I need something larger than a tongue right now.

"Problem?" he asks, eyebrow raised.

He's fucking with me. He knows what I want.

"I don't want that." I stumble over my words because he's just flattened his tongue and run it over the length of me. Thank fuck I kept that waxing appointment yesterday.

"No?"

"I want you in me." It's getting harder to talk, because he's good with his tongue. "I want you on top of me."

"Oh, I love the dirty talk, Boots. Go on."

His tongue is flicking my clit and I arch my back over the bed. I'm totally going to come like this, but it's not what I really want right now.

"I want your cock inside of me, Sawyer. I want you to sink it into me, with my legs stretched wide and all of your weight on top of me. And then I want to feel you move. I wanna feel you sliding out of me and then slamming back inside. That's what I want."

He flattens his tongue and sweeps it across my clit while inserting one thick finger inside of me and dragging it in the perfect come-hither movement. I come, thrashing my head on the bed and screaming his name.

I'm panting when he stands, wiping his mouth with the back of his hand. Jesus fuck. That move right there has another flood dampening my already wet pussy. He drops his pants and kneels on the bed, leaning over me to snag a condom from the bedside table. Propping myself up on one elbow, I wrap a hand around the length of him, running it up and down. I could weep with joy. It's a nice dick. Hard. Thick. Long. Did I mention hard?

I flick my eyes up to find him watching me examine his dick, which is hot, so I hold his gaze and twist my wrist, gliding my hand back and forth. He's thick, my fingertips barely touching. I've given enough handjobs, and I can usually rest the pad of my thumb on the nails of my fingertips as I stroke, but there's no overlapping here. I swallow, not breaking eye contact with him. The stretch I'm going to feel with him inside of me will be incredible.

I drop my eyes back to his cock in time to watch pre-cum escape the tip and I move my hand up to rub my thumb through it, then use the moisture to massage the head of his dick before dragging the tips of my fingers and thumb together over the head of his cock.

"You like that?" I ask.

A grunt escapes his lips, followed by a notable increase in his breathing.

"How about your balls?" I whisper, dropping my hand to cup his sac, then use my nails with the barest hint of pressure.

"Yes, I like that," he says, sliding an arm under my knee, knocking me flat onto my back. I grin and stretch my arms over my head, lifting my pelvis towards him. He watches me, slowly running his eyes down my torso while ripping the condom package with his teeth. He returns my grin with a lazy one of his own, then winks at me. He's kneeling between my legs rolling a condom on and he winks.

It takes the breath right out of my lungs. I'm not sure why that changes the moment for me, yet it does. It's inexplicably endearing. In the midst of this sexual furor, it says more than *I want you.* It says, *I'm having fun with you.* I think I could have fun with him for the rest of my life.

He aligns himself with my opening and glances at my face, then pauses.

"You good, Everly?" He says it softly, questioningly, his eyes fixed on mine.

I nod with the slightest movement of my head and suck my lip between my teeth when he slides the head of his cock inside of me. He's still kneeling, guiding his dick into me with one hand, gaze intent on the point where our bodies are joining.

It's been a while. I don't own a vibrator—living in a dorm room is not exactly conducive to that kind of privacy. I flex my toes and arch my back as he slides in deeper, my body adjusting to the oh so welcome invasion. He slips his other arm under my opposite knee so my legs are bent back, knees near my chest and toes pointing to the ceiling, and then he thrusts in completely.

A whimper escapes my throat and he pauses for a moment, letting me adjust before he moves. When I release my lip from between my teeth and exhale, he leans over me and braces his forearms on each side of my head, resting his weight on top of me. I drop my knees, heels digging into the mattress on each side of his hips, and wrap my arms around his neck.

"This is what you wanted?" he says, pressing me into the mattress, the smattering of hair on his chest abrasive against my nipples in a way that I feel all the way to my clit. The flat planes of his stomach are resting against my own, and the weight of him feels like heaven.

"Yeah," I whisper in response. "You feel nice."

He meets my mouth with his own for a soft kiss.

"You feel nice too."

His eyes are inches from mine, the tip of his nose nuzzling against my own.

I've had sex before.

I haven't had whatever is happening right now.

I swallow, my heart rate increasing, and not from passion.

His lips drop back to mine, softly tangling with mine until I flex my pelvis, wanting more. He raises himself, unwrapping my hands from his neck and twining our fingers together over my head. Then he begins to move. He rotates his hips and slides out of me, the glide lighting up every nerve ending inside of me, then drives back in with a force that makes me gasp.

I dig my heels into the mattress and meet his thrusts, our entwined hands pinned to the mattress keeping me from sliding towards the fabric-covered headboard. I don't doubt the force of his exertion would otherwise have me mobile. Our combined breathing and the slapping of his balls against my bottom is the only soundtrack in the room. He's so deep it hurts in the best way. I love the feeling of being stretched around him, all the way to the base. The trimmed hair around his cock provides a light scratch to my clit when he angles just right.

"I'm gonna come," I say, but I already am. My pussy tightens around him so hard it would hurt if he thrust, but he pauses a moment while my climax subsides, chuckling softly at my announcement that came after the event.

He withdraws, sitting back on his heels and dragging me to him, hooking both my knees over his elbows and sliding back inside of me. My lower half is elevated, his hands wrapped around my waist as an anchor to pull me onto him as he pushes into me. We can both watch from this vantage point, and I'm so wet I can see myself on the condom when he slides out and hear it when he disappears back inside.

I whimper, a bit unsure if it's hot or embarrassing, but Sawyer's not unsure. He groans, and it's primal and raw and he can't take his eyes off us. His hands are still gripping my waist. He moves one, dropping a thumb to my clit and working it with a skill I've never experienced. I come again and he joins me, shouting his release, stilling inside of me, then pumping his hips slowly until he's spent.

Twenty-Nine

I wake up sore and alone. Something clatters out in the living room so I know he's nearby, but I'm almost glad he's up. Almost. The stamina of that man is something to be reckoned with. I came five times last night before he was done. We'd finish one round, fall asleep talking—my head on his chest, his fingers in my hair—and then we'd wake and start the entire cycle again.

Shifting, I roll over and then sit up, pulling the sheet up and tucking it under my arms. It's a nice room. I'd guess it must be professionally decorated. Probably his mother, I realize, recalling that she's a designer. I can't imagine Sawyer used someone else. I've already seen the master bathroom—it's tiled in marble and contains a double-door entry. There's a walk-in shower that would make any dorm-living girl cry tears of joy. I'm definitely using it before he takes me home, that's for sure.

The bedroom is simply furnished, clutter-free. The headboard on the king-sized bed is fabric, and as I scoot back to lean against it I catch something on the nightstand, a can of Diet Sun Drop. I reach over and pick it up, finding it cold. Sawyer must have left it there just recently. I pop the top and take a swig as Sawyer appears carrying a tray, which, if my nose does not betray me, contains bacon.

"Do you want coffee too, or just the soda?" he asks, nodding to the can in my hand as he sets the tray on the bed.

"You made me breakfast in bed?" I ask, eyebrows raised. He's too much. I'm waiting for a camera crew to pop out and tell me I've been punked. Massively, irrevocably punked.

He drops his hands to the bed and leans in, stealing a kiss. "To be fair, I didn't cook. Ordering room service is one of the perks of living here." He stands and walks towards the bedroom doorway. "Coffee?" he reminds me.

"No, I'm good," I tell him, taking another swallow of my beloved soda. When he walks back in with a coffee for himself it hits me. "Do you drink Diet Sun Drop?" I ask, holding the can up for a visual before setting it down on the breakfast tray.

"No." He uncovers the plates on the tray, stacking the lids and setting them aside. "And to be honest, I half expected your pussy to taste like Diet Sun Drop based on how much of it you appear to consume."

My eyes widen and a flush heats up my cheeks as I bite my lip. He's managed to make me blush.

"I wasn't sure what you liked so I got you scrambled eggs, hash browns, bacon and pancakes. Or you can eat an egg white omelet with me," he says, digging in with a fork.

I pick up a piece of bacon and shove half of it in my mouth. "You know about my Diet Sun Drop addiction but not what I want for breakfast?"

He takes a sip of coffee. "Well, your mom didn't pick up when I called this morning, so I had to wing it," he says, pointing at the tray.

I gasp. "You did not call my mother to ask her what I like for breakfast at"—I glance at a wall clock over the dresser—"seven in the morning."

He holds my gaze for a long moment, his face giving away nothing, until he finally breaks out a smile and I sag in relief.

"Not cool, Camden."

"I learned about your soda addiction from your social media accounts. It's not hard to piece together someone's likes and dislikes if you look in the right places." He tosses a smirk in my direction. "Your Pinterest boards alone are a treasure trove of information."

"Um, are they?" I wonder what exactly is on all those boards and how embarrassed I should be that he's looking at them so intently. I pick up a fork and break off a piece of pancake then look at Sawyer. "So what does my pussy taste like?"

"Seventy-three seconds."

"What?" I ask, popping a bite of egg into my mouth.

"It took you seventy-three seconds to ask what your pussy tastes like."

I roll my eyes in his face. "So you toss out commentary on my pussy flavor and expect I'm not going to ask? You're a tease."

He swallows and shakes his head. "No, I fully expected you'd ask. I just had my money on it taking three minutes."

"Tease."

"It does taste a bit like Diet Sun Drop."

"Stop it!"

He holds up his hands and shrugs. "It does. Diet Sun Drop and Everly."

"Not an answer."

"It is. Sunshine, citrus, and a great cabernet sauvignon."

Well, that was an answer, and specific enough to have me blushing again. I drop my face to the plates spread before us and take in his boring egg white omelet.

"Why are you eating that?" I ask. "If you were any fitter I wouldn't be able to walk today. Surely you can handle a pancake?"

He pats his abs, clearly on display since all he's wearing is a pair of grey sweatpants, and the movement distracts me. "I've gotta stay fit to keep up with my younger girlfriend."

"Do you typically date younger women?" I'm curious.

"No," he says, then pops a grape into his mouth. "I haven't dated a student since I was a student, I can tell you that much."

"Why does my brother want you to stay away from me?"

"Eric?" he says, as if I have more than one brother. He looks confused by my question for a second then nods. "Look, Eric and Finn are four years younger than I am. They grew up asking me for advice. They got all their best moves from me. Hell, those little shits used to listen through the walls when I brought my high-school girlfriend up to my room—"

"Eww!" I plug my ears. "La, la, la, stop talking. I do not want to know any of this about my brother."

He stops and smiles, a dimple flashing in his cheek, mirth lighting up his eyes. "I'll talk to Eric."

I shoot him a look to kill and he clarifies.

"I'll talk to Eric and tell him how much I like you, platonically. I'll tell him how much I enjoy you, and make sure he understands I'm not using you for mind-blowing sex. It's just a bonus."

I shake my head. I am never winning this. "Can we be done talking now?"

"Why? Did you want to have more of the mind-blowing sex?"

"No, I'm too sore." I shift my bottom on the bed and cross my legs.

"Really?" His face flashes a look of surprise and he eyes me up and down. "Fuck, that's hot."

I ignore him and shove a piece of pancake into my mouth.

"So my performance put your worries to rest?" His lips twist in amusement.

I blink for a moment before all of my fears from the night before come flashing back to me. I have to force myself to swallow the pancake because I'm already laughing. "I was genuinely getting myself worked up," I agree, and I snort, I'm laughing so hard. Then I cover my mouth, the snort so funny to me tears leak from my eyes.

His head is tilted in fascination, watching me laugh.

"Yes, you're good at the sex," I say, composing myself. "I was worried," I admit, "you're too good to be true."

Concern flickers across his eyes and he frowns, looking away. "There is something I should tell you."

My eyes widen to saucers. I knew it. My mind races with possibilities—drugs? Arrest record? Wife?—before I spit out an apprehensive, "What?"

"The thing is," he starts, dragging his eyes back to mine, "depending on the market, I'm not technically a billionaire.

Most days my net worth is still in the millionaire category."

"Oh, my God. You're an idiot." I groan and laugh, flopping back onto the bed.

"Honestly, the money is a hassle most of the time."

"A hassle?"

"Draws more attention than I'm interested in, truthfully." He rubs his forehead. "Investors, media, security." He drops his hand. "I'm not interested in being a Wikipedia page, you know?"

I nod. I can understand that.

"And my future children, I already wonder if I'm going to have to send them to the playground with security. Shit, I know I will. They'll be worth too much. Do you want children, Everly?"

"I do," I say carefully. "Of course I do. But I'm twenty-two. I want them in the future, and not the three- to five-year future, but the five- to seven-year future. I want to be settled first."

"Settled how?"

I take a sip of soda and think about how to explain it. "I want to be married for one. I want a wedding that is about us as a couple, and not timed around a baby bump."

He nods for me to continue.

"My parents are really happy, you know? And I want that for my children. I want to bring them into a secure relationship and I know there are no guarantees in life, I do. But I can make the right choices now to set the odds in my favor. Most of my friends' parents were divorced or miserable. Everyone had all these half-siblings and step-siblings and depending on custody weekends, sometimes the only time they saw each other was at school. It was hard."

"Life isn't always that neat, Everly."

"I know. I do. But I can at least try to get it right."

"We will," he says, then stands and carries the breakfast tray out of the bedroom. I flop back and stare at the tray ceiling over the bed while I mull over his words. *We will*. I hear the water start in the adjoining bath, and then he's back asking if I'm ready for a shower.

"Nice place you've got here, by the way."

He looks around, shrugs. "It's convenient."

"Don't worry, I won't be one of those girls."

"Which girls?" He's confused.

"You know, one of those girls who throw a fit because you've had sex on this mattress before? Then demand you get rid of it and bring in a virgin mattress for us to fuck on?"

"Is that an actual thing?"

"Oh, it's a thing. Chicks do it."

He wraps a hand around my ankle and drags my bottom to the edge of the bed, causing me to yelp. "I think we've already determined that you're not like most chicks, Boots." He scoops me up to carry me to the bathroom.

"Hey!"

"Problem?"

"No." I shake my head. "I just realized you were joking last night about sex tapes being your kink."

"And you're disappointed?"

"A little bit," I admit, holding up my finger and thumb an inch apart.

He's still laughing at me when he walks me into the most perfect walk-in shower ever. All thoughts of sex tapes are gone about a minute after that.

Thirty

"So you're dating Sawyer, not Finn?" Sophie asks, her nose wrinkled in confusion.

"Yup." I nod and smile. "Hey, I did not see this coming either. I really thought my story ended with Finn, you know?" I look at her expectantly. We're at Grind Me, the coffee shop we both work at part time. The morning rush is over and I'm finally catching Sophie up on what's been going on the past few weeks.

"Well, I did notice your fascination with Finn seemed to be completely in your own head," Sophie says, refastening her hair tie.

I shrug. It's true. What can I say? I pull out a roll of register receipt tape and peel back the glue keeping it from unwinding, preparing to swap out the roll that's about to run out of receipt paper in the register.

"But there was no telling you anything," she says, waving her hands in the air, "you were so determined that Professor Camden was the one, even though he made about as much sense for you as my gay ex-boyfriend made for me."

"I'm very happy that I'm able to provide you with this smug moment," I tell her as I make a face at her and drop the new receipt roll into the register and start the process of feeding it through.

"How the heck did Sawyer convince you though? You're so stubborn."

"I am not."

She snorts.

I snap the register lid closed and turn to her, hands on hips. "I'm not stubborn, I'm just right most of the time. There's a difference." I blow out a dramatic huff.

Sophie sputters, puts down the cup she just took a sip from and covers her mouth with the back of her hand until she manages to swallow and regain herself. "Everly, you're wrong all the time."

"What? When?" I'm incredulous. Wrong, my ass. I tap my foot, waiting for proof.

"Well," Sophie starts. "One." She holds up a finger. "My ex Mike was not a nice guy. You thought he was nice."

"You thought that too!"

"Two." She holds up a second finger and waves it at me. "Professor Camden is not your soulmate."

"Already established." I wave my hand for her to continue with her case.

"Three." She's undeterred. "Boyd was not stalking me."

"He sort of was," I argue.

"Fine." She shrugs. "Boyd was not stalking me because he wanted to ask me out."

"I can't predict everything. I'm not a fucking magician. Jesus."

"Four." She's still counting on her fingers. Sigh. "Professor Brown did not kidnap you and chop off your hair to make a wig."

"Yet." That chick is weird. It'll come out. I examine the ends of a strand of hair I'm twirling. My hair is incredible. I'd want a wig of it too, I admit. But still, she's weird.

"And five." Sophie's waving her open palm around like a solo jazz hand while I glare and wait. "The iced grasshopper mocha did not put Grind Me out of business."

"I thought they were going to use actual grasshoppers," I mumble. Who came up with the name grasshopper to describe mint and chocolate? An idiot, that's who. "Anyway, I was right about Luke. He is packing a donkey dick. You admitted that." I'm all pointy-finger-in-her-face, delighted in my defense.

"And I wasn't wrong about the waxing." I cross my arms across my chest, vindicated. "Tell me he doesn't enjoy that." Who's smug now? This girl.

"Ahem." We both stop and whirl to find her boyfriend Luke standing at the counter watching us. He looks amused, but a little befuddled. Sophie turns beet red, her eyes wide.

"Hey, Luke, nice to see you. Coffee?" I ask while Sophie slides around the counter to greet him. I watch as he drops a hand around her waist and bends to whisper something in her ear that has her ducking her head and blushing again. They really are adorable, I think as I grab a paper cup and sleeve it.

I hold the cup in front of the coffee urns, stumped. Sophie always gets his coffee. I didn't even start addressing him until he started undressing her. Truthfully I just enjoyed watching while she fumbled over helping him every week. Not in a heartless way, I don't mean that. It was delicious watching them. She was so dazzled by him she'd almost trip over her own feet filling his coffee once a week. And Luke? His eyes would trail her every move while her back was turned.

I glance over at them again and sigh in delight. I'm so proud of her for fucking her gynecologist. That takes some guts and I have to admit it, I was wrong. When I bumped into her after her appointment at the student clinic last month and she told me the clinic doctor that day was none other than the well-dressed hottie who came in for coffee every Tuesday? Hell, I thought I'd never see his face in Grind Me again, or I'd never see Sophie's face while he was in the store. But look at them now. Adorable.

"Luke, which roast do you want?" I interrupt their murmuring, tilting the empty cup in their direction.

"I'll have the donkey roast," he deadpans.

I hold back a smile while Sophie covers her eyes with her hand. I'm impressed. I didn't think Luke had that in him. He's kinda serious. I fill his cup with dark roast because it's the closest thing I can come up with, and, snapping a lid on it, place it on the counter.

He leaves a moment later and I catch him swat her ass on

the way out. She returns to the other side of the counter with a dreamy look on her face before she sees me and remembers I outed her talking about his donkey dick in the first place.

"I'm never telling you anything again. Ever." She glowers at me, but I'm not too concerned.

"Please, you just made the old man's day."

"Stop calling him old." She rolls her eyes. "Sawyer must be about the same age? He's older than Finn, correct?"

"Older than Finn, younger than Luke," I quip, but she's back to staring off into space with a little grin on her face. She's got it bad.

Thirty-One

"Chloe, promise me you're not going to stay inside studying all weekend." I'm tossing things into an overnight bag while Chloe has her head buried in the laptop on her desk.

"Promise," she says, holding her hand up over her head with her fingers crossed.

"Ugh, Chloe."

"Ugh, Everly."

We stare at each other, neither of us speaking. Finally she breaks.

"There will be plenty of time for fun in a few months. After I've graduated and secured employment."

"Secured employment," I repeat. "You sound like you're sixty."

She leans back in her chair and sticks her tongue out at me. "Whatever. What are your plans after graduation?"

Shit. I have no idea. "Um, I'm gonna communicate stuff," I say and nod confidently.

"Have you checked the employment ads lately to see what you might be interested in?"

"No, Chloe, it's December." She's so annoyingly practical.

"Maybe Sawyer can hire you." She shrugs and I flinch. That's not what I want. I know she doesn't mean anything by the comment, but it stings. I'm not waiting around with a fantasy plan of Sawyer giving me a gratuitous job or proposing so I can avoid finding employment altogether. I am going to get my act together. I always do.

"I'll figure out what I want to do before we graduate, Chloe. I just don't know yet. I'm not like you. I haven't wanted to be a teacher since the first grade when Mrs. Stowe let you be her teaching assistant for a day."

"That really was the best day ever," she agrees with a happy sigh.

I toss the Louboutins into my bag and dig through my drawer for my black lace bra. I know it's in here somewhere.

"What are you and Sawyer doing today?" She holds up a hand. "Besides the obvious. I already know he's going to fuck your brains out. Blah, blah, blah." She's turned to face me, both feet pulled up to the chair and her arms wrapped around them.

"We are going to the Reading Terminal this afternoon," I tell her, naming an old railroad station in downtown Philadelphia that's been turned in part into an indoor farmers' market of sorts. "After that, I don't know." I sit on the edge of my bed and grin. "But probably sex."

"Well, have fun." She scrunches her nose. "Wait, I'm not sure that 'have fun' is the appropriate thing to say to that."

"Oh, it's appropriate. We have a lot of fun," I respond, stressing the word 'lot.'

"I don't need any visuals, thank you."

"Why won't you just let me set you up with someone, Chloe? I bet his office is crawling with great guys. I already saw one who's super hot, but Sawyer's assistant has been pining for him for like, an eon, so I have to make that happen. But I'm sure there's loads more."

"No." She shakes her head, but she looks a little sad. "No, thank you. You've done enough to assist with my dating life."

I exhale in frustration. You put someone on a dating site one time without their knowledge and suddenly they don't want your help anymore. She's so unreasonable.

"You know, Chloe, in my experience sex is even better after college."

"You're still in college, Everly," she responds, practical as ever.

She's adorable in sweatpants and a waffle-weave long-sleeved tee. Her hair is piled on her head, hints of red weaving its way through the mess. She's sexy in the most unassuming way. And I really need to get her laid.

I wave off her dispute with a flick of my wrist. "You know what I mean. With postgraduate men."

"Postgraduate men? Formal much?"

"Your hymen is going to grow back together, Chloe. That's all I'm saying."

"It is not. That is not a thing," she huffs.

"It's a thing," I counter, then stand and hunt through my panty drawer to look for the lace panties that match the bra.

She's silent, but I hear the tapping of the keys on her laptop.

"Is not," she comes back with a moment later.

"But you looked!" I point a finger to the ceiling in triumph, certain this proves my point.

"Is Sawyer really that much better than anyone else you've slept with?" She bites her lip, her brow creased, as if it cannot be possible that it would be *that* different.

"I promise you, yes. I liked sex before, and I've never had bad sex, but…" I pause and search for how to explain it. "It's so much better, Chloe. It's better. I like him more, obviously. But it's more than that. It's more than this connection we have, which is spine-tinglingly phenomenal." I pause again, thinking. "Even if I didn't like him, the sex would be mind-blowing."

Chloe watches me speak, chewing on her lip again, her head tilted to the side and her nerdy little study glasses swinging from her fingertips.

"Okay," she says finally, and I'm satisfied. Because an 'okay' from Chloe is not a dismissal. An 'okay' from Chloe means she's heard me and she's thinking about it. I nod in contentment that I've done my part to ensure her hymen does not grow back together. Because that is so a thing.

Thirty-Two

Sawyer's waiting for me in the lobby when I get downstairs. He always waits. He parks his car, gets out, and comes inside for me. No pulling up and idling at the curb for him. And it's not because I'm running late. If I get downstairs two minutes early, he's already there. It gets me a little wet.

He's observing the shenanigans of Stroh Hall again as I walk up. I'm in comfortable clothes today—the cutest patterned leggings, boots and a snug-fit, white long-sleeved tee. I'm already zipped into my lightweight down coat when I get to the lobby, my weekend bag slung over my shoulder. Sawyer takes it from me as soon as I walk up.

He's in jeans and his grey pea coat, the collar of a cream-colored shirt exposed at the neckline. I could lick him, he looks so good. He smiles when he sees me and it stops my heart a little each time I see that smile again. His dark hair is rumpled, as if he showered recently and didn't do much else to it, but on him it works. Perfectly. I tilt my head up to him in greeting and he leans down to kiss me, but I grab hold of his jacket so he can't pull away.

"I have to tell you something," I whisper conspiratorially.

"What's that?" he whispers back, his eyes shimmering with interest.

Around us, the normal chaos of dorm life ensues. I think I hear someone skateboarding followed by a voice booming, "Not inside." The mailboxes snap open and closed behind us but still, I pause a beat.

"I want to do dirty things to you," I finally say, looking him dead in the eye and winking before releasing his jacket.

He responds with one of his lazy grins that spread across his face in wonder and end in a dimple on his left cheek. He doesn't say anything, just ushers me out the front door to his car. We're on 36th Street before he speaks.

"Tell me about it," he says.

I'm adjusting the seat heater on my side and it takes me a second to catch on. But once I do, it's on.

"I'd like to put your dick in my mouth," I respond. It's true, my mouth waters a little staring at his profile. I'm not lying when I say the thought of wrapping my lips around the girth of him turns me on.

His jaw tics, and he taps one finger on the steering wheel, but lets me continue.

I place my hand on his thigh, innocently enough. Mid-thigh, my fingers wrapping towards the inside of his leg, my thumb resting towards the outside. I don't move it up, just leave it there, my palm warmed by the heat of his skin, even through the denim.

"I'd wrap one hand around the base of you, get a good grip, and use the other to guide the tip of you onto my tongue. I'd have to stretch my mouth open pretty wide once I got the head past my lips." I pause and use a finger to rub along my bottom lip. "My jaw hurts just thinking about it."

We come to a stop at the light on Spruce and he turns his head in my direction, eyebrow raised in challenge.

"I'd like to deep throat you," I add, and, using my right hand, run the tips of my fingers down my neck, "but that is just not going to be possible with what you're packing."

He places his hand over mine on his thigh and squeezes. The light changes and he accelerates.

"I'd be happy to slide my cock past those lips of yours. But not tonight."

"What? Why?" It comes out a little shocked, and, if I'm honest, whiny. Is he saying we're not having sex today? Because I really want it. I've been thinking about it all morning. Fine. All week.

"Relax, Boots. I'm still going to fuck you."

"Whew." I exhale a giant breath and he just glances over and shakes his head.

"Can I fuck you without a condom?"

"No way. But I'll suck you off without a condom. And I'll swallow."

"Well, then."

"Hey, that's a good offer. I haven't swallowed since high school."

We're stopped at the light, making a left onto 22nd Street, and he glares at me.

I scrunch my nose and grimace. "But perhaps you didn't need to hear that."

"Perhaps not."

"Oopsie." I shrug. "Anyway, why can't I suck your dick tonight? You're being unreasonable."

He bites the inside of his cheek to keep from laughing at me. We're on Market Street headed towards Penn Square and I wait while he pulls the car into the Ritz-Carlton garage, slides into his parking space and gives me his full attention. He puts his arm across my headrest and traces the shell of my ear with his fingers before speaking softly.

"Because I want to come inside of you, even if it's in a condom. And then I want to do it again. And again. I don't know if I can hold off a load for your throat until tomorrow."

I want to blow him in this car right now, but I'm guessing he's a few years past that stage in his life. Plus it's a very tiny car.

"But I promise I won't bring you home tomorrow night without letting you suck my dick. Deal?"

"Deal," I agree. "But the Eagles are playing the Cardinals tomorrow, so I'm only available for a blowjob at half time."

"You like the Eagles?" His eyes light up in interest.

"I love them. I used to watch games with my dad every weekend when I was growing up." I laugh. "You can thank Finn for that."

"How so?" He raises a brow in question.

"He showed up at our house one time when I was, I don't know, around twelve, wearing an Eagles jersey. So of course I told him how much I loved football."

"Of course you did."

"I'd never watched a game in my life. But Eric heard me telling Finn how much I loved football, so he retaliated by telling our dad how I was dying to watch the games with him every Sunday." I shrug. "I ended up loving it."

He grins. "I gave him that jersey. Finn never cared about anything but running."

"So you've been unintentionally messing with my life for a decade," I mock complain.

"I'd have intentionally messed with you given the chance." He frowns. "Scratch that. Thank God I didn't meet you before now. Eric would've killed me."

"Probably," I agree.

His blue eyes glint in the dim light being cast from the parking garage lights and the tiny car manages to feel even smaller than it is. He's almost overwhelming, something I'm not used to. I'm usually the one overwhelming people, not the other way around. He makes my heart race in the best way, but I can't help but worry that this relationship is too easy, Sawyer's too perfect, and that the other shoe is going to drop at any moment.

Thirty-Three

We exit the parking garage hand in hand and walk past City Hall heading for the Reading Terminal Market. It's less than half a mile away, just a couple of city blocks. It's just cold enough to put a little hustle in our steps, but not enough to make it unpleasant.

The moment we enter through the 12th Street entrance, we're assaulted with the usual market pandemonium. Crowds of people, both tourists and locals alike. Smells competing from all corners of the large space. Shopkeepers offering samples lined up in front of their stalls. It's bedlam and I love it.

"Let's get ice cream." I tug on Sawyer's hand and nod my head towards Bassett's, rolling up on my toes in excitement.

"Ice cream? It's noon, we haven't even had lunch."

I stop dead and look at him in disbelief. "You buzzkill."

"We can get a pint to go later," he suggests and I take a step back.

"Whoa, buddy. I'm not sure this"—I point between us—"is going to work out."

He rolls his eyes and lets me drag him to the Bassett's line. We're jostled by the crowd as we shuffle our way forward and I examine the menu. I bounce on my toes again, peering over people's heads at my choices. Cherry vanilla, maybe. Mango, no. Not in the mood for mint chocolate chip. "Raspberry truffle," I tell the kid behind the counter with confidence when we get to the head of the line. "Sawyer?" I look over my shoulder. "What do you want?"

"I want coffee," he replies. I just shake my head and after grabbing my cone we backtrack to Old City Coffee and get Sawyer a coffee.

"Happy now?" I ask as he takes a sip and I swipe my tongue around the ice cream where it meets the cone. "Got your boring coffee."

His eyes follow the path of my tongue before he answers. "Not boring. This is quality small-batch coffee. You're the one missing out."

"Am I?" I ask, and now that I know he's so fascinated with the path of my tongue I make a dramatic sweep across the top of the cone while tilting my head back to look him straight in the eye.

"Cute, Boots. Real cute." He taps the tip of my nose with a fingertip and then grabs the hand not holding the cone and we set off into the crowded market.

We wind our way up and down the aisles, starting on the Filbert Street side and working our way towards Arch. I find a cookbook and a kitchen timer my mom will love for Christmas while Sawyer picks up a piece of pottery for his mom. We stop for cheesesteaks at Sparto's: Provolone for him, Whiz for me. Table space is limited so we find a corner and eat them standing up, Sawyer wiping a dab of Whiz from my cheek with his thumb.

After we've eaten, we continue shopping. Sawyer picks up steaks for dinner, with a final stop at Beiler's Bakery to pick up fresh-baked pastries and bread. The line at Beiler's is long, but I'm content waiting, leaning against Sawyer's chest and watching the bakery staff hand-roll donuts as the line shuffles forward. Through my contented haze I catch a couple of different women checking out Sawyer, and it's not the first time. Not even the first time today. I can't blame them, but it does give me pause.

I recall Finn commenting on me taming Sawyer or something like it. I think of Eric's reaction to Sawyer and I dating, before we were actually dating. He's calmed down a bit, but still.

The blonde ahead of us in line takes another look at Sawyer and I stop leaning on him so I can turn around and face him, sliding my arms around his waist and pulling him closer.

"What?" he asks, palming the back of my neck and massaging his fingers across my skin.

I drop my head back enough to look at him and release one arm so I can point a finger in his face. "Just so we're clear, you're mine."

He smiles in response. "You're such a little cavewoman."

"I'm serious."

"You're bewitching."

We stare at each other in a silent standoff until he leans down and kisses me. "Yours," he agrees when he's done. "But I thought I made that clear when I hacked your Facebook."

"Cute, Camden."

Thirty-Four

"Everly, honey, what time is Sawyer coming over?"

It's Christmas Day and my mom is bouncing around the kitchen, seemingly stirring a pot on the stove, mixing a bowl on the counter and popping a tray into the oven all at the same time.

"He'll be here by four for dinner, don't you worry." My mom loves to feed people and she's ecstatic about my new boyfriend. I don't think I've brought anyone home since the summer before college, come to think of it. No wonder she's excited.

I pry open the Tupperware with all the Christmas cookies and start arranging them on the platters Mom's got laid out.

"He said he can't wait to try my lasagna!" Mom boasts and I drop a cookie on the floor.

"What's that?" I ask, bending to pick up the cookie and toss it in the trash.

"He said you're always raving about my lasagna recipe." She beams. "I had no idea you liked it so much, Everly, I'd have made it for you every school break." She gives the pot on the stove another stir, knocking the wooden spoon against the edge twice before resting it on the spoon rest next to the stove.

"Um, when was this, Mom?" I tilt my head and pinch the bridge of my nose, my ponytail swaying with the movement. "That you were chatting with Sawyer?"

"Oh, we weren't chatting. We were Facebooking. On the FB."

"Mom, it's Facebook, not the FB. And you shouldn't be Facebooking my boyfriend, it's weird."

"I know it's just Facebook, Everly. But it's funnier to call it the FB, don't you think?"

"No." I'm shaking my head. "Not so much."

"Anyway, he messaged me."

I stifle a groan. I'm going to kill him. I wonder if Facebook has a feature to report this. I could care less about risqué pictures on my timeline. This? This I care about. "What else did you two message about?" I ask, my voice high as I close one container of cookies and pry open another.

"Nothing, Everly. He sent me a message to ask what he could bring today. That's all."

"That's all," I repeat.

"And I sent him some pictures. You were such a cute kid. It's been forever since I had anyone new to show those pictures to." She pulls a cutting board from the cabinet.

"Mom!" I shriek in horror.

"Joking, Everly. I'm joking." She shakes her head and pulls vegetables from the fridge, placing them on the cutting board. "I've never seen you so wound up before." She grins at me, her eyes sparkling. "He must be different."

I move my head in a slight nod. "He's something," I agree, as the door rings. It's too early to be Sawyer, but the relatives have started to arrive. My brother Eric will be here with his wife, Erin. My grandparents, an aunt and uncle and two cousins will be here too. I hear my dad opening the door to let whoever's arrived first in. At least Eric won't make a scene about me dating Sawyer in front of the relatives. I hope.

My teenage cousin Vivian bounds into the kitchen a moment later squealing and hugging me. She's graduating from my old high school Ridgefield High this spring. She takes over the cookies and updates me on all the schools she's applied to and where she's hoping to go to college next fall. I listen and take over the salad prep from my mom, feeling like it was a lifetime ago when I was in her shoes. Except of course, I only sent in the one application, so dead set that I would be accepted to Penn and everything would work out like I'd planned. I was right about getting into Penn, but wrong about everything else.

"What are your plans after graduation?" Vivians's finished her updates and looks to me expectantly, swiping a cookie and stuffing it in her mouth.

"Um, I don't exactly know yet," I admit. "But I've got time to figure it out." I smile and wave it off like it's no big deal. As if it doesn't cause me a moment of worry.

Vivian nods, a frown across her forehead. "Sure you've got time." She nods encouragingly. "I don't think I've ever known you not to have a plan though," she says, laughing as the front door opens, Eric and Erin arriving.

Eric arrives in the kitchen a moment later and points a finger at me with a simple, "You."

"Leave her alone." Erin's on his heels and slips an arm around his waist, fitting her head onto his shoulder and patting his chest with her free hand while he continues to scowl in my direction.

The door rings as we have a stare-off and my dad opens the door and says, "Nice to meet you." There's only one person coming tonight my dad's never met.

"Even better," Eric announces with a smirk and whirls back to the front door.

My eyes widen and I drop what I'm working on in the kitchen and wipe my hands on a towel as I take off behind him. He's going to cause a scene. This is mortifying, and I don't do mortifying. It was one thing when Eric messed with my high-school boyfriends, but this is something else altogether.

Erin and Vivian slam into me as I get to the hallway and stop. "Damn it," I whisper. Sawyer and Eric are already outside. Talking.

"What's going on?" Vivian whispers in response.

"Your cousin's lecturing Everly's new boyfriend on his intentions," Erin fills in as we all file into the living room so we can spy on them through the front window.

"Why?" Vivian asks.

Erin shakes her head in disbelief. "Eric's worried about Sawyer's playboy past. Like Eric didn't get around plenty before he met me."

"Eww, Erin!"

"Oh, sorry." She blushes.

Outside they're doing the bro back clap so we beat a hasty retreat back to the kitchen.

Vivian snorts. "Your brother is so overprotective. Like worse than your dad."

"We put it in his allowance," my mom announces and we all turn to stare at her, watching as she slides the lasagna into the oven next to a roast that's already baking. "He got a bonus for cockblocking you."

"Mom!" I'm not sure what's more horrifying, what she just said, or hearing the word 'cockblocking' come out of her mouth.

"Joking!" She flashes a grin at us.

I groan. When the hell did my mom become a comedian?

Eric and Sawyer walk into the kitchen a moment later, all smiles. Sawyer kisses my mother's cheek and hands her a bottle of wine, thanking her for inviting him. She actually blushes under his attention.

"That's your new boyfriend?" Vivian whispers to me, eyes wide.

"Yup."

"Damn, girl." She's openly eyeing him head to toe and I elbow her in the ribs.

Sawyer turns his megawatt smile on us next and I introduce him to Erin and Vivian before dragging him off to a quiet corner.

"What did you say to my brother? He looked like he was going to kill you, then poof, you're having metaphorical cigars together." I cross my arms and stare up at him, conscious that we're not really alone.

"Easy," he says, leaning down to my ear, his breath on my neck causing a shiver to run through me. "I told him I'm in love with you."

"Oh," I stammer. Oh. Am I supposed to respond to that? Now? With my family a few feet away? I'm fairly certain my eyes have widened to owl-like proportions and I dart my eyes back and forth wondering how much privacy we have, then suck my bottom lip between my teeth as I wonder if I can sneak Sawyer up to my room without getting called out for it. Which would be ridiculous, I'm twenty-two, but I'm not gonna push my luck with Eric.

Sawyer's eyes trace my face and he grins at my obvious distress before leaning down and touching my forehead with his.

"You can tell me how you feel about that later, Boots."

I release the breath I'm holding and nod at the same moment my mom calls out, asking Sawyer what he'd like to drink.

Drinks and appetizers pass without incident. Sawyer has everyone in love with him and my grandmother confides that he's quite the 'hotsy-totsy' and she'd give me a run for my money if she was a little bit younger. So I'm feeling pretty relaxed when we sit for dinner. That feeling lasts until the first bite of lasagna has passed Sawyer's lips and he raves to my mother about how long it's been since he's had homemade lasagna, with a little wink my way.

"Everly can make it for you! She's seen me do it a dozen times!" She beams with happiness as I choke on a crouton. "She has the recipe."

Sawyer pats my back but the dimple flashes in his cheek as he fights back a smirk. I clear my throat and take a sip of water.

"That's really sexist, Mother. Maybe Sawyer should make lasagna for me." I kick Sawyer in the shin as I deliver this edict.

"Fair point, Everly." My mom nods. "Maybe you can make it together?" She brightens with this solution and passes the rolls to my dad on her left.

"I'd be happy to make it for you, Everly." Sawyer jumps in. "I'll even drop it off at school. I'll call first," he adds without batting an eye. "Make sure you're in."

"How lovely!" My mom is positively glowing over Sawyer's perfection right now while I am plotting revenge. I am never breaking into anyone's apartment and making them lasagna again, that's for sure.

After dinner we gather around the tree in the living room, plates of cookies on the coffee table, mugs of coffee and hot chocolate all around. My younger cousin Bonnie distributes gifts from under the tree. Viv hands me a small package with a tag reading that it's from Sawyer. We're sitting on the couch next to each other, his arm wrapped over the back of the couch behind me.

I place it on my lap, waiting for Bonnie to finish passing around gifts, but obviously that's not going to do for everyone else.

"Open it," my mom prods. It's clearly a necklace box, and I slip my finger under the tape, then peel back the paper revealing a blue Tiffany box. I pop open the lid and start to laugh, which I don't want to have to explain, so I try to suppress the laugh and it turns into a weird snort. My mom gives me a funny look but must decide I'm trying to hold back tears instead of laughter and doesn't say anything.

"Pretty!" Erin leans over and examines the necklace and Vivian jumps up wanting a look.

"I'll put it on," I tell everyone, lifting it out of the box and holding up to my neck, leaning forward a little so Sawyer can clasp it for me.

"Keys!" Vivian says, getting a close-up look at the trio of silver keys hanging from a delicate silver chain around my throat. "Aww, that's so sweet," she coos and I try again not to laugh.

Of course he finds a necklace with three keys instead of just one. Of course. He tugs softly on the end of my ponytail so I'll look at him, and I do, his dimple firmly in place as he enjoys watching me try not to laugh. It's okay, he hasn't opened his present yet.

On cue, Bonnie hands him a box. It's about the size of a

shoe box, and I smile at him in anticipation.

He frees his arm from behind my neck on the couch and rips the paper off with abandon. He pops the lid open and digs through the tissue, pulling out a mug with a picture of a cat on it, and below that it says, 'I just freaking love cats, okay.'

"I'm taking this to work," he says with a grin.

"Oh, there's more, darling," I tell him, patting him on the knee.

He digs back in and comes up with a pair of silver cufflinks, shaped like cats. And finally, rolled up at the bottom, a tee shirt with a grey tabby cat wearing glasses and a backwards baseball cap. I grin from ear to ear.

"Do you have a cat, Sawyer?" Eric peers over, an investigative look on his face.

"No, but he really wants one," I answer before Sawyer has a chance.

Eric looks skeptical, like he suspects this is some kind of inside joke he shouldn't approve of, but he sits back without saying anything else.

"Sawyer, you didn't have to bring anything for me," my mom says, holding a flat package Bonnie has just placed in her lap.

"It's just something small; you might have them already," Sawyer says, leaning back and wrapping an arm around my shoulders again.

I am beyond curious as my mom delicately unwraps the present, and slightly fearful that it might be an inside joke that's going to poke fun at some ridiculous thing I've done and make me laugh.

"Oh, how lovely!" my mom exclaims, holding up what looks like a very old copy of *1, 2, 3 to the Zoo* by Eric Carle, followed by an equally old-looking copy of *Henry Huggins* by Beverly Cleary. "They're signed!" My mom is elated over any book, but Sawyer hit it out of the park with these two. "I'm surprised Everly admitted her namesake to you. She never lets anyone call her Beverly."

"And I'm not going to start," I affirm, "but I'll admit my name is adorable."

Sawyer's pretty adorable too, I decide.

Thirty-Five

"You throw a New Year's Eve party every year?"

I'm sitting on Sawyer's vanity, wrapped in a robe, watching him shave. I'm not sure how I've never watched him shave before, but it's definitely my new favorite thing. He's just gotten out of the shower, a towel wrapped around his waist, baring his chest, my other favorite thing. My poor eyes can't decide what to focus on.

"Yes. It's our annual party for the company."

"What if they don't want to hang out with you for New Year's Eve?" I ask, swinging my dangling feet. My toes are painted in Romantically Involved red. Fingers too.

Sawyer rinses the razor under the tap and then brings it back to his face and I am downright mesmerized. I clear my throat and shift on the marble counter.

"The party is optional, Everly. No one is required to 'hang out' with me. They can bring whoever they want, enjoy the free food and alcohol, or they can do whatever they want for the evening." He glances at me as he repeats the rinsing of the razor. "You okay there, Boots?"

"No, I'm kinda wet."

He glances down at the countertop surrounding the sink, devoid of a single splash, and then back to me. He tilts his head in question and makes another swipe with the razor.

"This shaving thing." I wave a hand at his face before fanning myself. "It's fucking hot."

He pauses, a towel in his hand, and shakes his head. "I

really am never sure what's coming out of your mouth next." He wipes the remnants of the shaving cream off his face and tosses the towel on the counter, dropping his hands on either side of my hips, caging me in.

"Neither do I, to be honest," I admit.

He's laughing as he tugs at my robe's belt and it falls open.

"No way," I protest, pushing him off. "I'm almost ready to go."

"I can't bring you to a party when you're horny. There's no telling what you'll do."

"My hair is done."

"I'll barely touch you."

I lean back against the mirror, dubious. "Barely?"

"One-handed," he replies, holding up his left, his right still planted on the counter next to my hip.

My robe is already gaping open and he slides the tip of his index finger from my belly button down to my clit. I gasp, and he knows he's got me.

"Feet up, heels on the counter," he instructs and I lift my knees, eager to comply. My eyelids are already heavy and I'm flushed with desire everywhere.

"Just the one hand?"

"A couple of fingers and a thumb."

My breathing increases as he slides his finger lower, circling my opening.

"You really are wet," he notes. He's standing over me, arm braced on the counter, our bodies only touching at the spot where his finger is rimming me. His face is less than a foot from mine, but he doesn't make any moves to kiss me or touch me in any other way. His finger slides in an inch and continues the rimming motion, the stretch satisfying. The contact is made more erotic somehow without him touching me in any other way. Our eyes are locked while he touches me so intimately.

He adds his thumb to my clit and I jerk. I feel his fingertip withdraw, then he's brushing it across my clit, paving the way for his thumb to return, smoothing the wetness around in small circles.

My breasts are heaving and I want a rough hand on them so badly. But he's resolved in his one-handed promise so I grab them myself. I'm not gentle, my hands cupped underneath, holding the weight of them, my fingers grappling at my flesh before pinching my nipples as hard as I can stand.

His thumb continues circling my clit as he drives two fingers into me, sliding deep. He tilts his wrist and drags his fingertips forward while pressing down on my clit with his thumb and I come, panting and incoherent. I grab his forearms with my hands, supporting myself as my toes bend over the edge of the counter and my back arches.

"Less than two minutes," he boasts, sliding his fingers out and holding up his hand. I can see myself coating his fingers, my eyes trailing their path to his mouth, where he sucks them clean. "One-handed," he adds, completely unnecessarily.

"Maybe I'm just a slut, you braggart," I call out as he heads out of the bathroom. I grab the towel he tossed on the vanity earlier and clean myself up, my thighs a damp mess. "You just made it worse!" I yell as he crosses the bathroom threshold.

"I know," he responds, tossing a grin over his shoulder.

I follow him to the walk-in closet. I've brought over half a dozen outfit options and they're all hanging in Sawyer's closet. He's already got his pants on and is buttoning his shirt by the time I get there. I drop my robe on the floor and then dig through one of the built-in drawers in the closet.

"Something I can help you find?" he asks. Because to be fair, I'm digging through his drawer.

"Nope," I tell him. "Found it."

"Everly, what in the hell are you doing?" He's finished buttoning his shirt and is staring at me, hands on hips, the corners of his eyes creased as he frowns.

"I'm putting on your underwear," I tell him, stepping into a pair of his briefs. I was digging around for a black pair. Why the hell do they even sell them in white? Just, no.

"Why?" He still looks bewildered, but he's stopped staring at me to tuck in his shirt.

"You got me all worked up and horny in there." I point a thumb in the direction of the bathroom.

"I gave you an orgasm." He seems confused by my accusation.

I snort. "Right. Which you know only makes me want your dick more." I glance over at the clothing I brought, contemplating what will work with this underwear. I've been chatting with his assistant Sandra all week about what people wear to this party. Sawyer was zero help on that front. "Wear whatever you want," he'd said. As if I can pick an outfit with that kind of direction. "I hope you're wearing your new cufflinks with that shirt," I tell him, eyeing his outfit of black slacks and grey dress shirt.

He holds up the cat cufflinks I gave him at Christmas and fastens his left sleeve. "I still don't understand what my underwear has to do with anything."

"Oh!" I pull a solid black sleeveless dress with a full skirt and a wide waistband off the hanger and step into it. "Because you're obviously planning on having your way with me at this party. Probably gonna shove me into a coat closet and fuck me with your hand over my mouth so no one hears us. And if anyone's panties are getting left behind at this party, it's gonna be yours."

He nods slowly and fastens his right sleeve. "Do women your age still use the phrase 'having your way with me?'"

"I just did. Anyway, yours are more absorbent. Can you zip me?" I turn my back to him and swipe my hair over one shoulder, waiting.

I feel his fingers on the zipper, the fabric gathering slowly up my back. He finishes and rests his thumbs on the back of my neck, rubbing small circles into my skin as he kisses the nape of my neck. I shudder, feeling his touch all the way to the black briefs. "That's a pretty elaborate plan I came up with," he murmurs.

I turn and nod, sadly. "I know. You're kind of a menace."

"It's good of you to put up with me."

I shrug. "Someone's got to."

"I'm not going to be able to rip those underwear off of you."

"Haha!" I point at him with one hand and slip a heel on with my other. "I knew it!"

He grins and shakes his head. "Never a dull moment with you."

"I do my best." I hop into the matching heels and head for the bathroom to add lipstick and finish fussing over my hair. "Thanks for letting me invite Chloe to the party." I dig the red lipstick out of my makeup bag and slide it across my lips, then, realizing this dress has hidden pockets, ditch the clutch I was going to bring and pocket the lipstick instead. "She'd stay in tonight and watch a *Criminal Minds* marathon if I didn't force her to come."

"No problem. I look forward to meeting her."

"Should I bring a condom or do you have it? My dress has pockets," I add helpfully.

He rolls his eyes. "Everly, we are not having sex during my annual company party."

"Right." I wink and nod my head. "Anyway, is Gabe coming?"

"Is Gabe coming?" he repeats back to me, a curious expression on his face. He leans against the door frame, arms crossed across his chest. "How do you know Gabe?"

"I don't," I huff, and dust additional powder across my face. "Is he coming or not?"

"He'll be there. You care why?"

"I'm working on something."

"You're working on something," he repeats. "Are you trying to set Gabe and Chloe up?" He doesn't look impressed.

"No!" Now I'm the one frowning. "That doesn't even make any sense, Sawyer." I smooth my hair over my shoulders. I had my hair professionally blown dry this afternoon. It's smooth and straight, hanging past my shoulder blades without a hair out of place. The red lipstick and nails are the only pop of color, contrasting against my dark hair and the black dress. I scoot past him in the bathroom door, checking the clock on the bedroom wall. "Are you ready?"

"Everly, what exactly are you working on?" he asks as we head out. The party is being held in the Ritz-Carlton ballroom, so it's a short walk to the party. Sawyer clasps my hand in his, this thumb rubbing over the back of my hand as we stroll.

"Getting Gabe and Sandra together," I respond, matter-of-factly.

He tilts his head in my direction. "Gabe and... Sandra?"

"Yeah, obviously. Why do you keep repeating everything I'm saying? Gabe and Sandra. It's so obvious."

"My assistant and my Finance VP are not a thing, Everly."

"Yet." I shake my head. "You are really short-sighted for an almost-billionaire."

"And you're a human resources nightmare." We're on the elevator and he rubs a hand over his jaw and closes his eyes.

"Wait, Gabe is your head of finance? I really had him pegged for a tech nerd."

"Because that matters right now?" He opens his eyes, looking bewildered.

"Oh, he's like one of the bosses! This just gets yummier and yummier." I bounce on my toes and clap my hands in delight.

"Everly, I don't think Gabe and Sandra are attracted to each other. I don't even think they're compatible."

My jaw drops and then I throw up a hand, palm out. "I've got this." I shake my head in disgust. How can he not see it? Then something occurs to me. "Does Gabe have a girlfriend?" I ask, eyes wide.

"I don't think I should encourage you by entertaining your questions."

"So that's a no. Good." I sigh in relief. We've reached the hotel tower of the Ritz-Carlton and we're taking another elevator to the second floor, the entire space rented out for the party. "Is he into kinky shit?" I ask in a whisper, my eyebrows askance. "What am I working with here?"

"Can we be done talking now?" He stole my line and he knows it, his dimple prominent as he gives me a wink.

"Sure." I shrug. "I've got it from here anyway."

We check in with the party planner running the event and Sawyer shows me around the space. Clemens Corporation has rented out the entire second-floor space. There's a buffet set up in the pavilion rooms. Multiple video games are set up with couches and candy buffets in both the rooms on the other side of the rotunda. A bar is open between the two rooms with small round high-top tables stretching from the balcony space all the way to the ballroom, which has music blaring and a live DJ. Another bar, a dance floor, waiters circulating with hors d'oeuvres and a variety of seating options cover the room. It's already the best party I've ever been to.

Then I spot Sandra and I remember I've got work to do tonight. Wait. What is she wearing? I blow out a breath as she approaches Sawyer and I, walking in her normal professional gait. Short, quick steps. No nonsense, chin up, back straight. And she's wearing a suit. A pantsuit, not even a skirt. She might as well be carrying a clipboard. Why does everyone always fight me so hard on my schemes? I mean, I know I didn't *tell* her my plans for tonight, but hello? New Year's Eve party? Is there a better time for her to attempt to get into Gabe's pants? No. No, there is not. I'm dealing with an amateur. I need to regroup.

We had lunch last week when I stopped by to see Sawyer and found out he was at a meeting in New York. I dragged her out with me, telling her I needed all the details for tonight's party and a fashion consultation. She'd told me it was an open dress code, meaning the guys showed up in everything from jeans to suits. The women mostly in party dresses, she'd said. So I'd thought we were on the same page.

She greets us both with a wide smile and tells Sawyer the party planners have everything under control and she has her cell phone if he needs anything, as always. He reminds her the office is closed until January third.

She's so pretty, her blonde hair pulled back low on her neck, blue eyes huge on her face, framed by thick lashes and eyebrows with a perfect arch. She's just shy, I decide, renewing the oath I've made to myself to get her under Gabe.

"Sandra, I forgot my lipstick back at Sawyer's. Walk with me to get it?" I pose it as a question, but I'm already grabbing her arm and turning her in the direction of the elevators.

"Everly, you put your lipstick in your—"

I whirl on Sawyer, the skirt of my dress twirling as I do, and make a motion with my fingers across my lips and mouth. "Zip it."

He throws up his hands and mutters something about finding a drink.

I loop my arm in Sandra's and make off for the apartment.

"Have you seen Gabe yet?" I ask.

"Mr. Laurent? No, he's not here yet. Did Sawyer need him for something?" she asks, but she brightens when she does and it tells me everything I need to know.

The elevator doors open in the lobby and we walk straight into Chloe, who, thank fuck, has worn what I put out for her before I left the dorm.

"Am I going the wrong way?" She's adorable when she's puzzled, her nose scrunched up, her forehead wrinkled. A wisp of hair falls from the arrangement on her head, falling across her eye, and she blows it away with an annoyed puff.

I drag them both back to the apartment and make a show of digging through my makeup bag looking for the lipstick that's in my pocket while Sandra hovers very awkwardly in the bathroom doorway and Chloe checks out the view.

"I don't think it's appropriate that I'm in Mr. Camden's bedroom," Sandra remarks, trying to keep her eyes on the floor.

"Relax, we just have normal sex in there," I tell her, gesturing to the bedroom. "It's not like we're making sex tapes or anything." I stop dead. Oh, holy shit, that's a good idea though. "Anyway," I say, drawing out the word, "found my lipstick. I guess we should head back to the party."

Sandra makes a beeline for the bedroom door while I take two steps then stop in front of the walk-in closet and gasp. "Wait!" She stops and looks up questioningly. Chloe doesn't even blink, used to my dramatics. I dash into the closet and return, holding up a black sequined miniskirt. "You should try this on."

Sandra starts to respond with an, "Um," but I've already crammed the skirt into her hands and shoved her towards the bathroom.

"Go on," I tell her, smile wide and reassuring.

"Uh, okay," she agrees. Her voice is reluctant but she's eyeing the material curiously.

She slips back out of the bathroom a minute later, still in her suit jacket but wearing the skirt. I'm surprised to see she was hiding some fuck-me heels under those pants. I can work with this.

"Sandra, your legs! I'd kill to have long legs like yours. You have to wear that skirt. I insist."

"You think?" she questions, walking back into the bathroom to look at her reflection. "I'm taller than you. This is really short on me."

"Yeah, I know. You're welcome." Gabe's not gonna be able to take his eyes off her. "Now take off your shirt."

"Excuse me?" Her eyebrows shoot up in question.

"Just the shirt under your jacket. Then put the jacket back on."

"Um, you want me to go to the party without a shirt?"

"Just do it," Chloe says, walking over from the window. "Or we're never leaving this room. Trust me."

Sandra twists her lips and does as she's told, reappearing in her suit jacket and the short sequined skirt. Perfect. The suit jacket is black and tailored, the cut creating a v-neck and exposing some skin, but covering plenty. Her legs look a mile long, bare under the short skirt and ending in those fuck-me heels.

"We should curl your hair," I announce, walking into the bathroom and plugging in an iron. She doesn't even fight me on this. Progress.

I sit her at the vanity in Sawyer's bathroom and go to work putting big loose curls into Sandra's hair.

"Who is Everly trying to set you up with?" Chloe asks her, while digging through my makeup bag, so she misses the startled expression on Sandra's face.

"What?" Sandra's eyes dart over to Chloe.

"She's setting you up, you know that, right?" Chloe, finding my hand lotion, looks up.

"I'm not setting anyone up." I shake my head. I'm not. I'm merely creating opportunities.

"She put me on a dating site without telling me." Chloe squeezes some lotion out of the tube and rubs her hands together. I don't think she needs the lotion. I think she was just looking for an excuse to rub her hands together in glee over having someone new to share my wrongdoings with. "Sent me on a date I didn't even know I was on," she adds.

"One time. That happened one time." I unplug the curling iron, wrapping the cord around the handle.

"Just make sure it doesn't happen again."

"It won't!" I promise, shaking my head.

She holds my gaze for a second, then nods.

"The thing is," I say slowly, testing the waters, "he's not here tonight, but I do think I found the perfect guy for you."

I'm met with a blank stare. Chloe doesn't even blink.

"You know how you have a thing for FBI agents?" I ask, getting a little excited. I wasn't joking about the *Criminal Minds* marathon. She's seen every episode at least twice. I take her silence as encouragement. "He's based here in Philly and he's hot."

Silence.

"And he's, um, tall. He's tall." I nod. Oh, God. I'm babbling. Chloe is scary when she's quiet. "And he's Irish!" I remember. "You would have the cutest babies." That was probably too far.

"So what's his name?" Chloe turns to Sandra, ignoring me completely. "Or do you even know? Sometimes she makes up things in her head that aren't actually happening. Is there a guy you like?"

"His name is Gabe," I answer for Sandra as we exit the

apartment, choosing to focus on tonight's goal instead. There's plenty of time to work on Chloe's love life. "He's not her boss, because I'm dating her boss and that would be super awkward, but he's a vice-president at Clemens Corporation, which makes it a little bit naughty, don't you think?" I don't wait for anyone to answer me. "Sandra wants to do dirty, dirty things with him on his desk."

Sandra blushes and shakes her head before stopping herself. "How could you possibly know that? You've seen us together one time."

"I'm observant." I shrug.

"Well, it's irrelevant," she says, straightening, spine straight as we walk. "It's not appropriate. And I'm not his type," she adds in a soft voice.

"We'll see about that," I respond. We've made it back to the hotel lobby and I spy the man himself waiting for an elevator to the party space on the second floor.

We'll just see.

Thirty-Six

"Gabe!" I call out cheerfully, waving when we've gotten a dozen feet away. He's about to step onto an elevator, but he stops, turning toward the sound of my voice. He smiles politely as the elevator closes and leaves without him. I'm sure he's trying to place me because Sandra's correct. I've only seen him once.

His eyes move from me to Chloe and Sandra, and as I'd planned, he does a double-take when he sees Sandra. Tonight might be easier than I'd thought.

Chloe pushes the elevator call button while Sandra covers the formal introductions. If Gabe thinks it's weird that I was calling his name across the lobby when I've not technically been introduced to him, he doesn't show it, likely because he's a little distracted with Sandra.

"So you came alone?" I ask as the four of us step onto the next elevator. Sandra and Chloe shoot me simultaneous looks of ire, clearly unimpressed with my segue from introductions to fact-finding.

Gabe glances in my direction, then back at Sandra. "I did."

I nod to Chloe with a discreet tilt of my head and widen my eyes, as if to say, *See, I was right.* Chloe tilts her head back and shrugs. She knows I'm right, but it'll kill her to admit it. I hope Gabe and Sandra have a big wedding so I can bring Chloe as my plus one.

"See you later!" I call out as we all step off the elevator on the second floor, grabbing Chloe's arm in the process. "I'm going to find Sawyer so I can introduce him to Chloe," I explain, and then I make a run for it. I imagine it's much the same way a mother feels when she drops her child at kindergarten for the first time. I stop the moment I find a hiding place so I can peek back and make sure Sandra's stayed put where I left her, with Gabe.

"He's totally into her. You see it, right?"

"Yeah, fine. He's into her," Chloe admits, begrudgingly.

"They're so cute they're going to need a couple nickname. Sabra! Sabra's perfect. Coined it!" I do a little raise-the-roof motion with my hands to celebrate my brilliance.

"Sabra is a brand of hummus."

Oh. Maybe not so brilliant then. I drop my hands and frown.

"He's hot," I observe from our vantage point. "The nerd glasses really work on him, don't you think?" He's dressed up tonight. The last time I saw him he was in jeans with his shirt sleeves rolled up. "He's wearing the hell outta that suit."

"I can't argue with that," Chloe agrees, peering around the corner with me.

"What is she doing?" I grumble. "Her flirting skills are atrocious."

"What did you expect her to do? Drag him into the coat closet?"

"I would love it if she did, but right now I'll settle for more eye contact. She's staring into her drink."

"Yeah, she is. Oh, no, incoming."

We watch as a tall blonde joins Gabe and Sandra, and we both groan when the intruder puts a hand on Gabe's arm and Sandra takes a visible half step back.

"You stupid bitch, take your hands off Sandra's man," I whisper, even though Chloe is the only one paying attention to me.

"He's not interested in the new blonde, look at him," Chloe observes.

"Of course he's not, but Sandra's gonna bolt in less than a minute. Just watch."

A throat clears behind us and we both straighten and turn, finding Sawyer directly behind us. He looks pretty comfortable, hands in pockets, standing inches away. I'm guessing he's been here a minute. He cocks an eyebrow at me before moving his gaze to Chloe.

"Everly's roommate, Chloe, I presume?" he asks, reaching out and shaking her hand.

"Sawyer, I've been looking forward to meeting you." Chloe is positively beaming. "I'm a fan of anyone who can give this one"—she nudges me in the ribs—"a run for her money."

Sawyer rubs his chin in a play of delight. "Oh, I bet you have stories. We should have lunch sometime."

"Ha, ha, you two. Ha, ha. You can exchange numbers later. We need to focus right now."

"Yeah, what have you done to my assistant?" Sawyer frowns, the corners of his eyes creasing as he takes in Sandra's appearance. "What happened to her pants?"

"She looks hot, right? You can admit it, I won't be jealous. Damn, her legs in that skirt. I wish my legs were that long." I say wistfully.

"Are we calling that a skirt? It looks like a headband."

"Don't be old, it's a skirt," I assure him. "Gabe liked it," I add.

"He definitely liked it," Chloe agrees while I nod smugly.

"But now that meddling tramp is horning in on all my hard work," I say, waving at the unknown blonde who joined Gabe and Sandra. And then Chloe and I groan in unison. Because Sandra has just given up and left Gabe and the new blonde. She's wandered over by the balcony, looking miserable.

"Go keep her company while I strategize," I tell Chloe, and now Sawyer is the one groaning.

We circulate, everyone wanting to stop Sawyer for a quick hello. Chloe and Sandra disappear into one of the game rooms set up on the other side of the rotunda separating the party space, and Gabe watches her go. He detaches himself from the unknown blonde, but he doesn't follow Sandra.

"Getting other people laid is hard," I complain to Sawyer

the second we're alone. He grabs a glass of champagne from a passing waiter and presses it into my hands.

"Maybe you shouldn't interfere," he suggests.

"No." I shake my head. "I don't think that's going to work." I take a sip and tap my fingers against the glass. "Do you have any ideas?" I look up hopefully.

"Hmm." He tugs at his ear, appearing deep in thought, then he looks at me and deadpans, "No."

"Well, you should."

"I should?"

"Yeah, you were plenty creative in bulldozing me."

"I like to think of it as wooing."

"Well, it was effective. So where are your ideas now? When I need them?"

"I'm not sure if I'm comfortable being involved in your plans to get my assistant laid."

"People getting laid are fifteen percent more productive than those who are not."

He stares at me for a second. "You just made that up."

I nod. "It sounded pretty good though, didn't it? I thought it sounded pretty good."

"Well, you're getting laid plenty, Boots, so I'm sure you'll think of something."

Damn. He really outmaneuvered me on that one.

"Walk with me," I tell him, sliding an arm behind his back. "Have I told you how handsome you look tonight?"

"You didn't spell it out, but I might have gotten the hint earlier."

"Super hot," I assure him, patting his back with my hand as we walk. Then I toss in a little, "Rawr," which might have been overdoing it because Sawyer belts out a huge laugh.

"Everly, you're shameless. And really, really transparent."

"Is it so wrong to want to help?" I ask. "Sometimes people just need a little push. Or, you know, a really hard shove. Or possibly to be accidentally locked in a closet together." I glance around the room, wondering if I could pull that off tonight, but quickly decide I don't know the layout well enough.

It turns out Sawyer knows the layout just fine, because I'm in a supply closet with his hand under my skirt a second later.

"I knew it!" I cry. "Knew it, knew it, knew it."

He kisses me, likely to shut me up about being right about the party sex, but I got my boast in so I'm not going to complain. Then he backs me up to the wall beside the door and uses both hands to pull the briefs that I'm wearing under my dress to mid-thigh, and then I'm not really thinking about being right anymore.

"If you finger me and don't follow through with a hard fuck I'm going to kill you," I warn, wrapping my arms around his neck and pulling his lips back to mine.

He palms half my ass with one hand, holding me firm while a finger from his other hand circles my clit twice before sliding quickly inside of me.

I bang the back of my head against the wall and sigh in pleasure.

"You don't want me to make love to you in this closet, Everly?" He thrusts his finger in hard, in contrast to his words. "You want a hard fuck?" His finger retreats and then he slams two in. I gasp and my knees buckle slightly, but between the wall and his grasp on my ass, I'm not going anywhere.

"Yeah. Fuck me hard, Sawyer," I manage to cry out. "Please."

It's dark, a crack under the door providing the smallest sliver of light, but not enough to make him out by. I feel his mouth on my neck without seeing him move, the darkness and the party just outside the door adding an erotic element I'm not used to.

"I love how wet you get." His mouth is at my ear now, his lips barely touching me, his breath caressing with each word. "You're ready to fuck in under two minutes," he murmurs, and I get even wetter than I was a moment before. I run my hands down his arms, gripping his biceps through his shirt, as I clench below around his fingers.

He groans and pumps me again, his movements rough. I like it, and I move my hips to push back against his hand. I'm warm everywhere, standing in this closet in a sleeveless dress. My body is flushed with heat, my nipples are tight. I'm hyperaware of every inch of my body and every inch that he's touching. I rotate my hips again, grinding myself against his hand, my chest heaving and my pussy aching for more.

"I'm going to fuck you in this closet, Boots. With six hundred people just outside the door. You like that?"

I nod, before realizing he can't see me. "Yes. I think I do," I whisper in return. "Is that okay? That I want you to fuck me like this?"

"It's more than okay," he grunts.

"It's not too dirty?"

He laughs. "No."

"Then I want it." I trail my hands down his forearms then move them to his waist, tracing my fingers along the belt until I make out the buckle and slip it open, the ends hanging as I quickly undo the button underneath and then slide his zipper down. "I want your cock inside of me. Right here, right now."

I reach into his pants and pull him out, wrapping my palm around the length of him in the process. I jerk my arm, masturbating his erection with my hand. He slides his fingers out of me and wraps his hand over mine, tightening my hold and increasing the pace. I can feel myself on his hand, wet against my skin. It feels filthy to be jacking him off like we're teenagers in a closet after a round of spin-the-bottle with friends in the other room, rather than a corporate party that he's hosting just beyond the door. But it feels powerful too, knowing he's in here with me, my hand wrapped around his dick, my arousal coating his fingers.

I slide my wrist out from under his and cup his balls with my hand. He continues jerking himself off, his breathing rapid and a groan emitting from his mouth when I drag my fingers over his sac in a clawing motion.

"Turn around," he orders me. "Hands on the wall."

I pivot around, my legs still trapped mid-thigh by the underwear, and rest my palms against the wall. My heart races in the darkness, my thighs damp, my ears straining to make up for the lack of sight. I hear the crinkle of a wrapper and the brush of fabric as he wraps himself. Then the skirt portion of my dress is flipped over my back and his hands are firm on my hips, his fingers squeezing solidly into my skin. He drags me backward a foot until I'm bent over, hands on the wall and ass up.

His feet are bracketing mine, the fabric of his slacks smooth against my bare legs. He has to bend to line up. I can feel the friction of the fabric against my legs before I feel him at my entrance. He nudges inside of me, and I moan softly. I love the feeling of him being inside of me, even an inch. He slides both hands forward, his palms warm against my stomach, fingers interwoven, and then he lifts me to the tips of my toes and thrusts deep at the same time.

I gasp and call out his name, my palms pressing against the wall securely to keep my balance.

"You okay?"

I breathe in and out for a second. "Yeah. It's really deep. You're really deep." I wiggle my hips. "It's good."

He withdraws several inches and I close my eyes. The slide is so good. I don't think I'll ever get tired of the feeling of him inside of me. He's so thick and long and being this full drives me wild, the slide of his cock splitting me open my personal nirvana. He presses into my lower abdomen with his hands, pulling me onto him as he drives in again, and I almost come right there. Holy shit, the pressure of his hands against my stomach, combined with him inside of me, it's too much.

I mumble something and he stills, sunk as far as is physically possible inside of me. I feel his stomach against my ass, the fabric of his pants against the backs of my thighs, and I'm reminded that we're fucking in a closet during a party.

"Still okay?" he asks.

"Yes." I sigh. "The thing with your hands, it's good."

He presses firmly against my stomach, the heel of one hand dragging across my skin, and thrusts again.

"That. Oh, my God, Sawyer." I shove on the wall, pushing back on him with the only leverage I have, and he starts to fuck me in earnest. The sound of the party is a backdrop to the slaps of skin against skin and the rustling of clothing inside the closet.

My head drops forward, my hair a curtain around my face. I can make out our feet from the fragment of light coming under the door. Polished black shoes planted on the floor outside of the tips of my heel-clad ones, barely touching the ground. I watch my toes rock back and forth as he slams into me from behind and it's so deliciously dirty.

"I'm close, Sawyer," I tell him, clenching tightly around him, increasing the drag of his cock as he slides backward. "Fuck me as long as you want. I have to come," I warn him, trying to keep my arms firm on the wall as I climax.

"That's quite the offer, Boots," he responds as he slows, but does not stop. He thrusts slowly through my orgasm, my body pulsing around him, the friction increased from my muscles contracting around him. I feel every bit of it with his deliberate slide.

"Sorry," I pant. "Sorry I came so fast. Holy fuck, Sawyer." My chest is heaving with exertion, even though I'm doing almost nothing but holding my upper body off a wall. Sawyer's doing all the work on this one. "Do you want a blowjob or do you want to keep going?"

He pounds into me from behind, the smack of his skin against mine renewing my desire like a whip.

"No, I don't want you on your knees on the tile floor in a hotel closet, Everly."

Shit. He's so sweet.

Then he fucks me so hard I worry about the safety of my wrists and I end up with both forearms pressed against the wall to keep my head from cracking into it.

He comes with a husky grunt, stilling as he presses me into the wall, his body pressed along my back for a long moment, before setting me down on my feet and withdrawing.

"I'm turning on the light."

There's a light?

I squint, the warning doing nothing to help my eyes adjust

to the sudden invasion of light. I grumble, leaning against the wall, annoyed I have to stand right now. I want to lie down on something soft while Sawyer runs his fingers over my naked back and I fall asleep with my head on his shoulder. Instead I have to pull myself together and slip back into this party.

Sawyer wraps his fingers around the base of the condom and slides it off his cock, then ties it off into a knot. He's still partially erect. I love watching his dick, seeing it in all its various states. It fascinates me. I love that he doesn't care—he's not shy about my curiosity in the slightest. I asked him to come on my tits last week just so I could watch. Not shockingly, he was happy to oblige that request.

I couldn't take my eyes off him, watching him masturbate, knees on either side of my hips. His arms—fuck, those arms. His biceps flexing as he held himself over me, jerking himself with one hand, rougher with himself than I ever am with him. Then he came, erupting onto my chest, and I didn't know where to focus. On his face, watching me while he did it, or the actual release onto my skin. I mean, I don't ever get to see *that*.

The look on his face when I ran my hand through it, spreading it over my tits, well, that was a look that will be embedded into my memory forever. And a moment later when he tossed my legs over his shoulders and stuck his face between my thighs... well, I think he enjoyed it too.

He pockets the condom and zips himself up, then turns to me. "You okay there, Boots?" There's a smirk on his face that indicates he knows damn well that I'm fine. Well fucked, but fine. He closes the distance between us and nudges my chin up with his finger, then presses his lips to mine. "There's a bathroom around the corner," he says, straightening my hair with his fingers before bending and pulling the underwear still around my thighs up to my hips.

I nod and he grabs my hand before killing the light, then walks us back into the party like he owns the place. He walks me to the ladies' room and I have a fleeting thought wondering if he's ever fucked anyone else in that particular closet before deciding that I don't care. I don't give one fancy fuck who he's been with, I've got him now and I'm keeping him.

I enter the bathroom and head straight for a stall to clean myself up, but I'm waylaid by Chloe and Sandra sitting in the lounge portion of the ladies' restroom. I've walked into a conversation and a sad Sandra.

"Oh, hey." I wave and eye the stalls across the room.

Chloe frowns and eyes me slowly. "At the party, Everly? Really? He lives like ten feet away. Jesus."

Sandra's eyes widen as she glances between us, getting Chloe's meaning.

I shrug and head for a stall. "You've seen him, right?" I call out. "His place is much too far away when he looks like that."

"Oh, God," Sandra replies behind me.

"Be thankful you don't live with her. Weekend update takes on a whole new meaning."

"I can hear you!" I call from behind the door.

"I know!" Chloe calls back.

I finish and wash my hands then walk over to where they're sitting, hand on hip.

"Hey, it's all fun and games now, but who do you come to when you want to know if it's normal for a guy to come in under a minute?" I point to myself. "Me. That's who." I raise an eyebrow in challenge.

"Yeah, yeah."

"Now"—I turn my attention to Sandra—"why are you two hiding in the bathroom?"

"We're not hiding," she says, slumping on the sofa. "We're just sitting for a minute."

"Come on." I step forward and hold out my hands to each of them. "Get up." I pull them up and then stop at the mirror next to the door to freshen my lipstick and smooth out my hair. "I didn't get you all sexed up to hide in the bathroom. Let's go get Gabe."

Thirty-Seven

We exit the bathroom. Sawyer leans against the banister surrounding the rotunda behind him, speaking with a couple of people I don't recognize.

"I'll meet you guys in the game room," I say, nodding to the room next door that's set up with video games. Then I slide in next to Sawyer, his arm going around my waist the moment I'm close enough. He introduces me to a couple of guys I won't remember in an hour as I spy Gabe at the bar.

"I need a drink," I tell Sawyer as soon as the guys leave our sides, keeping Gabe in my line of sight.

"I'm sure," he replies dryly. But he doesn't fight me on it, instead walks me straight over to Gabe, standing at a tall table near the bar with a brunette. She needs to go, obviously.

The guys shake hands and I immediately see the ease between them. They're friends, I realize. I give Sawyer a little side-eye glare. He could have provided me with this information earlier.

"You've met my girlfriend?" He nods to Gabe and introduces me to the brunette. I'm given her name at this point but I promptly forget it. I'm sure she's a lovely girl, but no. She needs to find someone who is not Gabe.

The guys delve into sports talk while I drum my fingers on the tabletop, strategizing. "How long have you two known each other?" I interrupt when I catch something about rowing come into the conversation.

"Since Harvard," Gabe replies. "Roommates,"

"Uh-huh," I respond. I flick my eyes over to Sawyer and he smiles.

I smile back as I pull my phone from my dress pocket. "Oh," I say, frowning at the screen. "Oh, my." I hold a hand over my mouth in faux shock and flash wide eyes at the table, catching the amused expression on Sawyer's face as he waits for whatever stunt I'm about to pull.

"Sandra isn't feeling well," I announce. "Headache. Gabe"—I turn to him, placing my arm on his sleeve, eyes imploring—"could you drive her home?"

His eyes widen in surprise at my audacity, then he grins, glancing towards the room that Sandra went into a few minutes ago. The glance is so brief I almost miss it. Then his eyes are back on mine and he rubs his fingertips across his temple. "Sure, sure," he agrees, then a moment later, "She needs a ride?" he asks, even though he's just agreed to give her one.

I nod with what I hope is an earnest expression. "She does." Then I type out a rapid text to Sandra, informing her she has a headache and Gabe is driving her home.

A flash of annoyance crosses the brunette's face as she realizes any plans she had for seduction tonight will not be realized. Her eyes take one last hungry sweep over Gabe before she excuses herself. Bye, Felicia.

"Hey, remind me to update you when we're back in the office," Gabe says, nodding to Sawyer as he turns towards the room Sandra last went into. "Our guy has a new lead in Los Angeles. He thinks he's close."

Sawyer flexes his jaw and runs a hand down his neck, but nods as my phone dings with a reply from Sandra.

WHAT?!?!

He's headed towards you now.

I don't even have a headache!

No kidding. I recommend putting out, but you do whatever you're comfortable with. Have fun!

I pocket my phone with a satisfied smile as Gabe enters the room Sandra's in.

Sawyer shakes his head, a look of resignation on his face. "I should really get better control of you," he mutters.

I snort. "If you'd wanted a controllable girl you'd have never gone after me."

"That's fair," he agrees with a wink.

"Did you notice he never even asked where she was? Because he knew. Because he's been keeping an eye on her all night!" I point my finger in triumph.

"Duly noted."

"Sandra is so getting laid tonight," I muse with a contented sigh.

He groans. "We're definitely done talking now."

Thirty-Eight

"Do you think a sex tape is an appropriate birthday gift?" I dump a cupful of ice into the blender on top of the milk-and-coffee combination I've already dumped in. I squint at the blender and then grab the chocolate syrup bottle and overturn it, making sure the chocolate is flowing before I glance back at Sophie.

It's mid-morning and the early rush at Grind Me is over. Sophie is refilling the napkin dispenser at the register while I mess with my creation in the blender.

"To clarify, you mean filming yourself having sex with Sawyer?"

"Uh, yeah. What else could I mean by a sex tape?" I dump a handful of chocolate chips into the blender and start peeling a banana.

She shrugs. "How would I know? Maybe you meant a celebrity sex tape. Or a tape of you working a stripper pole." She tosses me a cheeky grin.

I pause, frowning, then shake my head. "I don't have time to learn how to work a pole before his birthday so that's out."

"I was joking about the pole." Sophie pulls a box of straws out from under the counter.

I add the banana to the blender. "No, it was a valid suggestion. Maybe next year."

"Next year?" Sophie's ponytail whirls as she turns around and leans against the counter. "You're already planning gifts a year out?" Her eyebrow is arched, a smile on her face.

"I'm already planning gifts for the rest of our lives."

"All the shit you gave me about being too serious with Luke so quickly and you're head over heels in love with Sawyer in just over a month?" She's got her hands on her hips, head tilted in dismay.

"I was wrong." I shrug, and snap the lid on the blender.

"Huh," Sophie replies, once the blender stops.

"Huh, what?" I ask, dumping my drink into a cup and snapping a lid on it.

"Huh, I didn't think you'd admit defeat on that so quickly."

"When you're wrong, you're wrong." I hop up onto the back counter and stuff a straw into my drink. "Holy shit, I'm a genius. Taste this." I hold out the drink to Sophie, wiggling my wrist back and forth in excitement. "So good!"

Sophie takes the cup from my hand and sips, then grimaces and hands it back. "Disgusting."

"It is not!" I take another sip. "Who doesn't like chocolate and banana?" I'll admit, some of my concoctions are pretty bad, but this one is happiness in a cup.

"No." She shakes her head. "I like chocolate and bananas, but something is off about that." She points to the cup in my hand.

I glare at her and take a big obnoxious sip, causing an air pocket in the cup and a loud slurping noise that I encourage, wiggling the straw around. "Your taste buds are damaged or something."

"If you say so," she says, her expression indicating she thinks no such thing.

"Back to my potential sex tape, it's a good idea, yes?" I don't wait for an answer before continuing my case. "It's impossible finding gifts for a guy with enough money to buy anything he wants. And what man doesn't want a recording of himself banging his girlfriend? Every man wants that. Am I right?" I look to Sophie for confirmation.

"Sex tapes and anal. It's on every man's wish list."

I grunt. "Yeah, and I already told him I'm saving anal for marriage, so that's out."

"Wait, you've never had anal?" Sophie's eyes widen, her voice a whisper.

I glance at her face and slap my drink down on the counter. "You have?" I'm stunned.

She darts her eyes away from mine and then back, biting her lip and nodding, her face red.

"How is this possible? You were a virgin five minutes ago and you've already progressed to anal?" I shake my head. "Oh, my God. I'm an anal old maid." I drop my forehead into my hand with a slap, then sit up straight, my hands gripped around the counter's edge as I lean forward to get Sophie's attention. "Did you like it?"

Sophie clears her throat and glances around again, like someone is going to catch us discussing this and post about it on Facebook. "Yes," she whispers, then looks at the ceiling as if she can't meet my eyes while she admits it. "It's, um, good. I don't want to do it every day, but occasionally, yes, I like it."

"Huh," I say. "Well, then."

We get a customer then, so Sophie helps them while I sit on the back counter and Google sex tapes with my phone, which, as it turns out, does not give you instructions about how to make a sex tape, but instead pulls up links to sex tapes that have already been made. I change my search to *making a sex tape* and get similar results. Has no one made a blog entry about this? I mean, where do I start? Can I use the camera on my phone? Do I need industrial lighting?

I tap the side of my phone with a fingertip and sigh, watching as Sophie adds sprinkles to a hot chocolate for the little rugrat peering over the counter, its mother standing nearby stirring cream into her coffee. It's kinda cute, I decide. *She's* kinda cute, I correct myself. Moms probably don't like it when you refer to their kids as *it*, even in your head.

"I hope my ass looks that good after I have kids," I comment, watching them leave, hand in hand.

"First forever, now babies?" Sophie jokingly clutches her chest. "My heart can't handle it."

"No." I snort. "Don't be stupid. First forever, babies in a

decade. And trust me, my happily ever after does not involve a surprise pregnancy. Not happening." I wave my hand in the direction of the door. "She was cute though. I'll babysit for you and Luke."

"Funny." Sophie laughs. "Real funny."

The door dings again and I look up to see Sophie's brother walk in. He's wearing a suit, and I catch a glimpse of the badge clipped at his waist when his jacket flaps open from the wind as the door swishes shut behind him. I have got to finagle a way for him and Chloe to meet, I muse as I call out a hello and then turn my attention back to my fruitless internet search on sex tapes while Sophie and Boyd chat at the register.

Then a thought pops into my head and I look up. "Boyd!" I call out excitedly. You should always use your resources.

They stop talking and look my way, twin expressions of inquiry on their faces.

"Do you know how to make a sex tape? Like, specifically? I get the sex part," I say, waving my hand, "but do I need a special camera? Or a tripod or something? Do you know?" I ask earnestly, scratching a dry spot on my knee.

"Everly!" Sophie snaps in response.

"What?" I ask, confused. "Look at him. Odds are he's filmed it a time or two."

Sophie's eyes bug out. "Do I need to remind you that you have a brother?"

"I know I have a brother. I'm not going to ask him for advice on making a sex tape. That's disgusting." What is wrong with her?

Sophie shakes her head. "Yeah, and that's *my* brother," she says, pointing at Boyd and making a face at me.

Oh. Yeah.

"Well, can you wait in the back room?" I ask, wrinkling my nose. "There's a shocking lack of information available on the web." I hold up my phone as way of proof. "Sawyer's birthday is in a week."

"Please stop talking," Sophie says, holding up her hand in a stop motion.

I sigh and look at Boyd, who is looking at me like I'm nuts. He really is perfect for Chloe. I might need to work on that anonymously now, come to think of it.

I shrug and change the wording of my internet search. That's better. I smile at the new search results and start reading.

Thirty-Nine

"Where the hell is Sawyer? We're going to be late for our dinner reservations." I'm leaning against Sandra's desk looking at the clock on the wall. I've been hanging out in Sawyer's office for fifteen minutes. I don't mind waiting, but it's weird. He's always so punctual.

"I'm not sure. He had me cancel everything this morning and he's been in and out of his office all day," Sandra says. "It's not like him."

I look at the clock again and then back at Sandra. If we're late to dinner I can roll with it. It's Sawyer's birthday. I'm sure whatever he's doing is important.

"So." I grin at her, eyebrow raised. "New Year's Eve?" I leave the question hanging in the air for a minute. "You got home okay?" I prod when she doesn't answer.

Sandra flushes and nods, not meeting my eyes. "I did," she admits.

"That's it? That's all I get?" I ask, laughing.

"I, um…" She taps her mouse, bringing her computer to life, and clears her throat. "Thank you," she finally offers, then swivels in her chair to face me and says, "I got home very well." Then she grins, bites her lip and swivels back to her computer screen.

Sawyer walks in then, firing off directions to a well-dressed woman in her forties walking beside him. He's almost rude, his voice sharper than I'm used to hearing from him. He says something about seventy-two hours and not a moment longer while she nods with a, "Yes, Mr. Camden."

He notices me then, leaning on Sandra's desk located outside of his office, and surprise flashes in his eyes the second before he recovers and stops short, clearly remembering just now that we have plans. That it's his birthday.

"That'll be all, Marlene," he says, dismissing the woman without even looking at her. "I'll expect an update from you with the test results in the morning. Sandra will see you out."

The woman doesn't appear bothered in the least at the abrupt dismissal. She smiles kindly at Sandra, who has popped up and collected her coat from the closet outside of Sawyer's office. So she's not an employee, whoever she is.

I follow Sawyer into his office and pause, unsure what to do, when he drops into the chair behind his desk, the view of downtown Philadelphia to his left. He drops his forehead into his hands, elbows bent on the desk in front of him. He sighs, rubbing his face with his hands, and I stand, hesitant. I've never seen him this stressed out.

"Sawyer?" I ask, tentatively, and his head snaps up. He drags his hands though his hair then smiles, some of the tension leaving his body.

"We have dinner plans," he states, motioning with his hand for me to come closer.

"For your birthday," I remind him, closing the distance between us. I slide between him and the desk and hop up to sit on the surface, resting my hands on his shoulders. "Everything okay?"

"Yeah, yeah." He rests his hands on my thighs, but it feels like an expression of comfort as opposed to copping a feel.

"You still want to go?" I ask, massaging his shoulders. "I was gonna spend the night after. Give you your birthday present."

"Were you?" He grins, that dimple I love so much flashing on his left cheek.

"Yes." I nod, face serious. "It's too dirty to give to you at the restaurant. So it'll have to wait until after dinner," I whisper in his ear.

"I like the sound of that."

"Good."

I'm glad he's perking up. I got waxed today, I'd hate to waste it.

And my nails. I've painted them Porn-A-Thon peach. Toes too. You think I'm kidding? I spent an hour looking at nail polish names online before finding this one. Then I had to make a special trip to a department store to buy it.

But it's worth it to make Sawyer's birthday perfect.

"We should go," he comments, glancing at his watch.

I slide off his desk and stand. I'm wearing a navy jersey dress and it hugs my figure in all the right places. Sawyer finally takes notice of that when I'm on my feet and my chest is in his face.

"Or we could skip dinner," he throws out, placing his hands on my hips, his palms warm through the fabric.

"You know I'd normally take you up on that offer, but I'm guessing you skipped lunch today by the way it looks like your day went."

Something flashes in his eyes and I want to kick myself for bringing it up, but it's replaced by an easy smile a second later.

"You're right," he says, standing. I trail behind him to the coat closet in his office.

"Besides, you'll need your strength for later, tiger." I slap his ass as he's reaching into the closet to grab our coats, his back to me.

He's still for a moment, my view of his face blocked by the closet door. The door slowly closes, the hinge creaking in the otherwise silent office.

"Are you serious with that behavior?" he asks, head cocked to the side, expression neutral.

"Yup." I nod immediately and shrug my shoulders. I was serious, what else can I say?

He holds the impassive facial expression for another few seconds, his lips trembling by the end. Then he laughs and pulls me in for a kiss.

"What would I do without you, Everly?" His eyes search

mine, all the tension from before gone.

"You'd be crazy bored."

"Crazy," he agrees, sliding my coat over my arms.

We pass Sandra on the way to the elevators, returning to her desk from escorting Marlene out. I'm tempted to ask Sawyer about his day, curious about what had him so stressed out, but I feel like the mood broke back in his office and I don't want to get him stressed again, so I let it go. I'm sure he doesn't want to think about boring business stuff tonight anyway.

Forty

Dinner is perfect. Sawyer is back to his usual self—maybe a little tired, but that's to be expected after a stressful day.

Sawyer teases me throughout the meal, asking about his present, making wild guesses, asking if it's stashed in my bag or if I've dropped it off at the apartment already. I refuse to give him a single clue, laughing while he drums his fingertips on the table and comes up with one wrong idea after another.

"Geez, I hope you like it, after all this guessing. I hope you'll be into it," I add with a wink as the waiter approaches with dessert menus.

Sawyer declines the offered dessert menus and asks for the check without taking his eyes off mine.

"I'll be into it," he promises with a slow, sexy grin. His eyes roam my face, taking in every detail.

"I don't get dessert?" I ask, eyebrow raised.

"Nope." He's completely unapologetic as he shakes his head. "You can order whatever you want from the room service menu. Later."

We're outside minutes later, waiting for the valet to pull his car up. His arm is around my waist, and I'm leaning into his side when he presses a kiss to the top of my head and whispers, "I love you, Everly."

It's not the first time he's said it. And it's not the first time I've said it back, but it hits me in the gut, as heavenly hearing it now as it was the first time.

The car arrives, sliding up to the curb with a soft purr.

Sawyer grabs the passenger door and hands me into the car before slamming the door closed and circling the car to the driver's side.

"This car," I say with a shake of my head as we pull away from the curb, merging into traffic headed towards Penn Square. "I thought you were going to be such a dick, driving a Porsche."

"Yeah? A Porsche didn't say successful CEO to you?"

"No, it said player having an early mid-life crisis."

"You'd have preferred an SUV with a good safety rating for car seats?" He glances in my direction. "You've made it pretty clear that's not what you're looking for right now. Besides, I just turned thirty-five today. I've got at least half a decade until the mid-life crisis kicks in, no?"

"Well, I guess it's good that you're enjoying the car now, because by the time you're actually in the mid-life crisis zone, you'll be in an SUV filled with car seats."

"Yeah, maybe," he agrees, pulling into the parking garage at the Ritz-Carlton Residences.

We get upstairs and he's all over me the moment we walk in the door. He almost manages to distract me into a quick fuck in the foyer before I remember I have a plan and pull away.

"Your present," I whisper, placing my hands against his chest and giving a little shove to break the contact of his lips on my neck.

"I can wait," he murmurs, pulling me back.

"No more waiting." I laugh and give him a real shove this time, then grab his hand and lead him over to the couch. "Sit," I instruct, pushing on his shoulders till his ass hits the couch. "Give me your phone," I tell him, palm out.

He shifts on the couch, reaching into his pocket, and a moment later the phone is in my palm. I glance at it, an iPhone exactly like mine, and swipe the screen to life.

"Unlock it," I demand, handing it back. I have a moment of concern then, wondering if he's going to balk at giving me his phone unlocked, but he doesn't even pause. His fingers bump mine as he takes the phone back and keys in the code before placing it again in my outstretched palm, nothing but curiosity written on his face.

I clutch the phone in my right hand, holding it up, then place my left foot on the couch cushion next to his knee, leaning forward slowly. I assume he thinks he's about to get a little striptease based on my body language and the way he shifts back on the couch, relaxed, head tilted in my direction.

I lean all the way in until my lips are beside his ear. "Wait here," I purr before standing. I grab my purse from the front hall—I'm using a large tote style tonight to stash my goodies—before disappearing into the bedroom.

I turn on every light in the room as I strip, dashing into the bathroom to freshen up my hair and makeup. I leave those lights on too, for good measure. Grabbing the telescoping tripod from my bag, I toss it on the bed with the phone, then gather up the rest of my stuff, bringing it to the walk-in closet. I set my bag down and pull out the wisp of fabric of my one-piece lace bodysuit. The cut is high on my hips, the edging scalloped. The scallop detailing continues on the deep v neckline held up by the tiniest spaghetti straps. It's orange, a perfect complement for my peach-colored Porn-A-Thon nails.

Sliding into the bodysuit, I adjust the fabric over my tits and feel for my keys necklace, the only other thing I'm wearing. Perfect. Leaving the closet, I place my phone in the speaker dock on Sawyer's nightstand, hitting play on the playlist I created for tonight. Then, moving to the foot of the bed, I open the special telescoping tripod I ordered. It's got a clamp to hold the phone, similar to a selfie stick. It's a filthy selfie stick, basically. I clamp the phone in place, check the angle and press record. It's go time.

I open the bedroom door. Sawyer turns in my direction when the door latch clicks, so I extend one arm over my head, leaning against the doorframe, and beckon him to me with a flick of a finger from my other hand.

It's dark in the living room, but I can see Sawyer's face by the moonlight flowing in from the floor-to-ceiling windows spanning the length of the room, the William Penn statue visible in the view behind him. But I'm more interested in the view inside of this room. I watch his face as he takes me in. His eyes slowly roam from the top of my head to the tips of my toes and back again. He sinks his teeth into his bottom lip and smiles, his head tilting in a slight nod before he rises, walking slowly towards me.

He looks a little predatory as he closes the distance between us, loosening his tie as he walks. And even though we've been together many times, it makes my heart race with anticipation.

He reaches the doorway and I step back, drawing him into the room before he can touch me. He follows, tie undone and hanging around his neck, hands already undoing the buttons of his shirt, which somehow still looks fresh and crisp at the end of a long day.

I walk to the edge of the bed and pause, one knee brushing the comforter, then turn my head to see what he's doing over my shoulder. I'm momentarily distracted by his fingers, moving with precision downward, the fabric slowly parting, but snap my eyes up in time to see his reaction.

His eyes are firmly on my lace-covered ass so it takes him a moment to take in the tripod arrangement at the corner of the bed. He stops mid-movement, his suit jacket halfway down his arms, then chuckles.

"We're making a sex tape?" His jacket flies in the direction of a chair near the door, followed by his tie.

I turn fully and face him, the bed behind my knees, the camera recording, and nod my head. I'd ask if he was okay with the idea, but the expression on his face tells me the question would be a waste of time.

He closes the distance between us, sliding his hand behind my neck, lips crashing on mine. God, I love that move. His fingers are firm on my nape, warm against my skin, thumb under my jaw maneuvering the tilt of my head to the exact position he wants it in.

I moan into the kiss, my arms resting on his shoulders and my hands promptly finding their way into his hair. The pads of my fingertips dig into his scalp, trying to pull him impossibly closer.

He pulls back, and I catch his lip with my teeth, tugging softly for a moment before releasing him. His chest is heaving and his pants are already tight over his erection.

"This," he says, fingering the delicate strap on my shoulder that holds up the flimsy bodysuit. "You should wear this every day."

"I bought it for you."

"I approve," he murmurs, sliding one strap over my shoulder and following the path with his fingertips down my arm.

It makes me wet, just his damn fingertips running down my forearm. Okay, who am I kidding? My body is in a constant state of readiness whenever he's in the room. But then he touches me and I'm soaked.

"Buy it in every color. Wear it every day." He nudges the second strap down my opposite shoulder and the top half of the bodysuit falls to my waist. "Just not right now."

He runs his hands around my hips and smooths the scrap of fabric down my thighs until it's nothing but a pool of lace around my ankles.

I yank his unbuttoned shirt from his pants, pushing it back over his shoulders and down his arms, leaning forward and licking his nipple as I do. My tongue makes a wide, flat sweep across his skin and he grunts, flinging the shirt clear of his arms then grabbing a fistful of my hair to drag my lips back to his mouth.

He picks me up, my knees wrapping around his waist, and places me on the bed, following me down, our lips still connected until I'm horizontal, then he pulls away.

He stands up, taking me in lying naked on his bed, dragging his bottom lip between his thumb and forefinger. And Lord help me, that's a move I love too. He's not even touching me when he does it, yet my pussy clenches as if his hands are on me. Every time.

He glances at the camera then back at me as he undoes his

pants. His dick springs out, directly in line with the camera, and I'm already looking forward to watching that on playback. Repeatedly. He fists himself, pumping his erection, and my mouth waters. Is that normal? I can't help it—when he plays with himself right in front of me, saliva pools on my tongue and I have this urge to take him in my mouth.

I watch him for another moment, the muscles on his arm flexing as he strokes himself, then I flip my legs underneath me and kneel, wrapping my hand over his to still him, and circle my lips around the head.

Our hands are still wrapped together on his shaft as I flick my eyes upward to meet his. I alternate between swirling my tongue around the tip and sucking, my cheeks indenting with the suction, my eyes never leaving his.

I like the way his chest rises and his breathing hitches. I like viewing him from this angle. I like knowing that this powerful, beautiful man is thinking about nothing else in the world right now besides me.

He shifts his hand out from under mine and grips my hair, guiding me to take more of him. I glide my hand along his shaft, past the amount I can take in my mouth, and work him, my tongue and hand laboring in harmony together.

I squeeze my hand around him, stroking back and forth, and use my thumb to rotate small massaging circles on the underside of his cock where the skin meets his scrotum. I continue working him, bobbing up and down on him, my tongue and lips and fingers working together until he's spilling down my throat, his eyes on mine until the last moment when the pleasure becomes too great and his head tilts back, breaking our eye contact.

I pull back slowly, dragging my tongue across his cock from mid shaft to tip as I slide it from my mouth with a pop. I sit up on my knees, wrapping my arms around his shoulders, kissing his chest before he lays me on the bed, legs spread wide. He follows me down, his lips wrangling with mine before making a slow trail to his destination.

He loves going down on me. It drives me wild in all the

best ways. He's talented, to say the least. He keeps his gaze on mine as he kisses my lower stomach, a gleam in his eye, amused in advance at the pleading that will soon take place. I'm torn, every time. *Keep going. Stop. More. Less, please less. I can't take another swipe of your tongue. I surely will not survive it.*

He settles between my legs, my knees bent and splayed on the bed, his eyes still on mine as he uses his fingers to spread me open. His tongue is on my clit a moment later.

God, my heart is racing so fast.

I don't care what anyone says, a man giving oral is a different level of intimate than sucking a cock. I know it should be equal, but hell, their junk is hanging out all the time. Having his fingers holding me open while his face is an inch from my pussy, his tongue rimming my entrance, then his nose bumping my clit as his tongue dives inside, well. It's just not the same.

His lips brush against my sensitive skin, the added friction—even as slight as it is—making me fist his hair and buck my hips, begging for more, even as my mouth is spewing forth claims that it's too much.

He crawls over me, mouth crashing over mine. I can taste myself on him, and I like that too. Sex is messy if you're doing it right.

One of his hands cups a breast as the other reaches for the condoms in the bedside table. He's tearing it open when I place a hand on his forearm, stopping him.

"You don't have to," I say, glancing towards the condom in his hand. "If you don't want. It's not the right time in my cycle anyway." We've never had sex without a condom before. I've never had sex without a condom, period. But it's Sawyer.

An unreadable expression crosses his face, then he shakes his head and slides the condom out of the package.

"No, it's not worth the risk. I never should've asked that of you," he says, referring, I'm sure, to a conversation we had early on when he asked if we were going to ditch the condoms anytime soon, since I'm on the pill and both of us are clean.

I told him no.

Now I have a moment of surprise and a sting of rejection, if I'm being truthful, that he just turned me down. I don't have time to linger on it, because he's rolled the condom on and is nudging into me.

"I love you, Everly," he says, smiling down at me, that fucking dimple a shotgun to my heart. Then he slides into me an inch at a time.

I exhale a groan and tilt my hips up, welcoming him, my heels planted on the bed by his thighs, digging into the mattress for leverage.

He fills me, sinking into me until our bodies are flush. His hands slide under my back, his palms cupping my shoulders to hold me in place before he thrusts.

"I love you, too," I tell him, as he presses his forehead to mine and begins to move.

We stay like that throughout, my arms wrapped around his neck, his face inches from mine. Whispered words of lust and love from beginning to end.

After, I grab the phone from the tripod and lie with my head on his chest, arm extended so we can view the recording.

"Hmm, that didn't really go as I'd planned," I say sleepily, dropping my arm and stopping the playback with a flick of my thumb.

"No?" he questions, his fingers combing through strands of my hair and down my back.

"I think we recorded ourselves making love instead of the dirty hard fuck I assumed we'd document. It's kind of a shitty sex tape."

His hand stills on my hair, his lips pressing the top of my head before he speaks. "No, it's perfect."

Forty-One

"Good day student teaching?"

Chloe has just walked in, hanging her coat on the back of the door. She gets home every day after five, exhausted and smiling.

"The best!" She grins. "The kids are amazing. I can't wait till the fall when I'll officially be a teacher and have my very own class." She sighs happily as she pops a mug of water into the microwave to heat. "What are you working on?" she asks, nodding to the laptop open on my lap, notes strewn about me on the bed.

"Paper," I reply, closing the laptop with a snap. "It's not even due for two weeks. Impressed?" I tend to cram projects into the last minute while Chloe turns in assignments a week early.

"Whoa, hold on." Chloe peers out the window, looking at the sky. "Is it a full moon tonight? What is happening?"

"Ha, ha. Cute."

"No, seriously. What's going on? And why are you doing homework on a Friday night instead of getting ready for Sawyer to pick you up?"

"He cancelled. Emergency or something." I pull my knees up to my chest, wrapping my arms around them. "So I ordered a pizza and I'm working on a paper." I make a face. "Ugh. It's even worse out loud than it was in my head."

"Don't worry, staying in one Friday night won't make your hymen grow back together, I promise." The microwave dings and she dunks a tea bag into the mug of hot water.

"No, I don't think that's possible in my case. Sawyer's pretty big."

"I'm sorry I brought it up." She groans.

I cross my legs and plop my chin in my hand. I miss him.

"So you're not going over at all tonight? I haven't seen you on a Friday night in weeks."

"No." I shake my head, chin still in my palm. "Don't worry, I won't interrupt your *Criminal Minds* marathon."

"Okay." She grins, grabbing her laptop and tapping it to life.

"Is it weird that he cancelled?" I ask, giving voice to the nagging worry that's been bouncing around my brain for the last hour.

"I don't know, is it?" Chloe glances over at me then back to her keyboard, flipping through the options on her Netflix account. She selects an episode and sets the laptop on top of the microwave where we can both see it. She doesn't need to pay close attention since she's seen every episode already. Honestly, I think she just enjoys having it running in the background, the way most people enjoy music.

"I don't know." I twist a piece of hair around my finger and stare at her open laptop while I think. "We had a great time on Wednesday, his birthday. I slept over, he dropped me off on his way to work yesterday morning and I haven't talked to him since."

"So you spoke to him yesterday?"

"Yeah, I know." I nod. "I know it was just yesterday. But it feels off somehow." I give my hair another twirl. "Let's just watch your serial killer show and eat pizza."

Chloe grabs a slice from the box on my desk and sits on her bed, legs kicked out in front of her, totally content with a Friday night spent with her beloved fictional federal agents.

We're quiet for a few minutes, the show playing while Chloe catches up to me on pizza consumption.

"Why do you like this show so much? It's kinda dark," I observe, cracking open a fresh can of Diet Sun Drop.

"They're like a little family," she says with a shrug. "Hotchner's like the dad figure, he keeps them all together, you know? Morgan's crazy hot, kicking in doors on every episode. Dr. Reid is the most adorably awkward genius ever. Penelope's kinda like the mom. She stays behind at the BAU worrying about her team out in the world, but she's really running that whole operation, right? She's the glue. JJ proves you can be a pretty girl and still take out a bad guy with a single shot. And Agent Rossi's the one you'd confide in if you needed advice about a secret."

"So you haven't given this much thought then," I mock.

"You asked." She shrugs.

"You officially have an agent fetish."

"It's comfort television."

"It's a show about a group of FBI agents profiling serial killers," I say incredulously.

"Well..." She pauses, thinking. "It's comforting knowing they're gonna catch them."

"You're nuts."

She smiles and stuffs another bite of pizza in her mouth.

****

I wake up at ten the next morning and check my phone. Nothing from Sawyer. By noon the feeling of dread has settled firmly in my stomach. I could text him, sure. Call him, absolutely. Yet I'm not going to. Something feels off and I'm wondering why he hasn't contacted me. I open up the text chain between us and review the ones from yesterday afternoon. There it is, the last message from him that said, 'Talk soon.' Talk soon? It was weird to me yesterday but I brushed it aside. Because Sawyer and I are solid.

He's never given me a reason to doubt him, and I'm not a girl to go looking for reasons that don't exist. I might have doubted his intentions during that first car ride, when he drove me back to school from Ridgefield the Sunday after Thanksgiving. He chipped away at my doubts during that week of Sawyer-style wooing, ending with a goldfish complete with a fancy self-cleaning tank. I look at Stella, swimming happily in the mini-fish tank with Steve, and smile. Who does all that? Not a guy just interested in a quick fling.

From the day that I showed up at his office, I knew he was all in with me.

Until today.

He's had a stressful week, I tell myself. I'm being crazy. Paranoid. He's going to call any minute, tell me he's on his way to pick me up.

But he doesn't.

By late afternoon I pick up the phone. This is silly. Maybe he thinks I'm mad about last night? Maybe I'm making myself sick over nothing.

He doesn't pick up. I get a text a moment later. *Can't talk right now. I'll call you tomorrow.*

Okay then.

Not really. He's never sent me to voice mail.

He doesn't call the next day.

He texts me at 9 pm on Sunday. *I need some time, Everly.*

Is he fucking kidding me? I don't reply. I stare at the ceiling of my room all night, numb, drumming my fingertips against the bedspread, my mind blank.

By the following day my mind is anything but blank, thoughts racing, rethinking every encounter between us. I'm second-guessing myself and everything I know is true. I didn't imagine the last eight weeks, so what the hell just happened?

Forty-Two

"You're quiet today," Sophie remarks, wiping down the counter with a wet cloth and tossing it in the bin to be laundered. "And you're not making any horrible drink concoctions or stuffing your face with brownies from the bakery case." She tilts her head and looks me over. "What's going on?"

"I think Sawyer's trying to break up with me," I mutter.

"You think he is or you know he is?" Her eyebrows draw together in a frown.

"I don't exactly know." I cover my face with my hands and shake my head before dropping my hands again.

"Okay, Everly. What is going on? Did you have a fight?"

"No!" I shake my head, my ponytail whipping back and forth with the force. "Nothing like that. I saw him last week for his birthday. We made the sex tape. He seemed to enjoy that, then poof." I gnaw my lower lip, thinking it over. "He didn't want to fuck me without a condom," I tell her, glancing at her face.

"Um, does he normally use one?"

"Always," I say, glancing out the front window of the coffee shop. "But he's indicated before that he didn't want to use them. Then I offered and he turned me down. That's weird, right?" I glance back at Sophie, teeth worrying at my bottom lip again.

"I'm not sure," she says, shrugging. "Luke and I never use them anymore. Like, not since the first week or two."

"Seriously, Sophie?" I huff out a loud sigh of disapproval. "How many times have I told you? Two forms of birth control at all times."

"I think you've only told me that once," she says with a shake of her head. "And your admonishment is a little lost when you're in the midst of a story about trying to fuck your boyfriend without a condom."

"Well, there's that," I agree. "But it was going to be a one-time thing. Probably." I wave my hand. "Anyway, that's not the point. The point is that he turned me down. I'm not interested in having his illegitimate love child. Just what the fuck?" The sting of that refusal hits me again and my cheeks burn in mortification. I know I've done the same to him by refusing to have sex with him without a condom, but, well, that's my prerogative.

"I don't understand. You saw him last week and you haven't had a fight. Why do you think he's breaking up with you?"

"He cancelled our plans last weekend," I say and then pause. "Then he sent me a text saying he needed time." It's tough spitting that last part out. It's so stupid I want to punch him in the balls. Fucking time.

"Oh."

"Right. Oh."

"How did you reply?"

"I didn't." Sophie furrows her forehead in confusion at my response so I continue. "I have a sick feeling about it. Something is off, but I'm so pissed that he's not talking and instead sent me a lame text about needing time." I heave a breath out. "I'm sad, Sophie."

She nods as the coffee shop door opens and her boyfriend Luke walks in. Her back is to the door so I see him before she does. His eyes immediately gravitate to her, softening at a mere glimpse of her.

It makes the back of my throat burn like tears are imminent. So I swallow instead and plaster a smile on my face, calling out a hello to Luke.

Sophie beams and slides around the counter so they can kiss.

I watch because I'm me. Plus Luke's pretty hot.

Sophie returns behind the counter and fills a cup of dark roast for Luke, sliding a sleeve over the cup and securing the lid before placing it on the counter with a shy smile.

He reminds her about a hospital benefit they have to attend this weekend and I thank my lucky stars I'm not going because I'm bored just hearing about it.

"I bet you two fuck like horny little rabbits," I comment as the door shuts behind Luke.

Sophie just holds up her hands, palms up, and shrugs.

"I still can't believe you're dating a gynecologist."

"Someone has to," she says in her practical tone of voice.

"You don't think it's weird that he's on his way to the student clinic right now?" I push. "It's not like he's an ear, nose and throat doctor."

"Please stop talking."

Forty-Three

I leave work and head back to campus. I sit though an afternoon class but it's a huge waste of time. I don't retain a single word.

I head to the Clemens Corp building as soon as class lets out. I need to see him. Maybe this is all in my head.

The lobby is fairly deserted when I arrive. Sandra gave me a building ID weeks ago so I could swipe past the security turnstiles in the lobby. I have a moment of panic wondering if my badge will work, if it's been deactivated, how far this 'needing time' thing goes.

But the light on the turnstile turns green and I'm through. I take the elevator to the top floor, reminding myself that Sawyer loves me, that I belong here, but the sick feeling in my stomach won't be quieted. The elevator opens and I make my way to Sawyer's office, my heart in my throat. I don't even know if he's here. Maybe this was a stupid plan.

I find Sandra at her desk and Sawyer's office door open, the light on. I can't see into the office from here, but I'm hoping the light indicates he's in the office today.

"Hey, Everly!" Sandra beams a smile at me and that off feeling in my stomach subsides. It's all in my head, surely. Sandra doesn't think it's odd that I'm here. Everything must be fine. Then she adds, "Have you met him yet?"

I don't get a chance to respond because Sawyer is there, and honestly, he looks kinda pissed.

Sandra's eyes widen and she glances between us. The

movement happens in a fraction of a second, the kind of thing you know in your gut just happened but you'll question later, wondering if you're embellishing the encounter in your head after the fact.

"Sandra, tell Gabe I need to see him," Sawyer says.

Sandra nods and picks up her phone.

"No, don't call him. Find him and tell him," he snaps.

That was the most obvious ploy to get rid of her, ever.

Sandra blinks and sets the phone back down. She's rising from her desk when Sawyer nods to me, indicating I should follow him into his office.

I don't want to.

This was a bad idea.

I feel like I'm about to get simultaneously broken up with and fired.

We make it three feet into his office before his cell phone rings. He glances at it, then back at me, before stopping in the middle of his office and turning in my direction.

"What do you need, Everly? Why are you here?"

He says it in a tone I've never gotten from him. He runs his palms across his face and I can see that he's tired, not himself. He's in jeans and a light brown sweater. I don't think I've ever seen him wear jeans to the office in all the times I've stopped by. And I damn well know I've never been asked why I was here to see him. Not once.

"Are you serious?" I ask him, my voice rising. "What do I need? Why am I here?"

"Everly." He sighs and pinches the bridge of his nose as the phone starts ringing again.

My eyes dart over to the desk where the phone is flashing. His keys are resting next to the phone, jacket laid across the desk. He's either just walked in or he's about to walk out. It's late afternoon so neither option makes sense.

He walks over to the desk and glances at the screen, silencing the call, phone clenched in his fist.

"Everly," he starts again. "I can't do this."

I think I'm going to throw up.

"Do what?" I press my lips tightly together and tilt my head, eyes narrowed on him. "What exactly can't you do?"

"Us."

The blood pounds in my ears as soon as the word leaves his lips.

"Why is that, Sawyer?"

"We're going in two different directions, Everly."

He doesn't even look at me as he says it. Instead he walks to his desk, back turned to me until he gets behind it. His eyes are flat when they catch mine again, the desk between us. I don't move any closer to him, still rooted to the spot a few feet past the threshold.

The phone rings again and he turns the ringer off, placing it face up on the desk in front of him. He places both fists on the desk, his face expressionless.

"What directions would those be?" I press.

He pushes back from the desk, standing straight, his eyes distant. I've never seen him like this. I've always felt like I was standing in a ray of sunshine when I had his attention. I had no idea the sun was eventually going to set.

"You're a lot younger than I am, Everly. You need time to grow up. Figure out what you want to do with your life."

"What does that even mean? I know exactly what our age difference is and so do you. You've known since the moment we met. That hasn't changed. *Nothing* has changed."

He rubs his forehead with two fingers, thumb against his temple like he's fighting a headache. "I turned thirty-five last week. I reevaluated."

"You reevaluated?" I seethe. "You just reevaluated me out of your life? Just like that? You cannot be serious with the bullshit coming out of your mouth right now, Sawyer Camden."

"You have no direction, Everly," he says sharply. "You're graduating in a few months and you have no idea what you're doing with your life."

He knows that bothers me. He knows it.

"You selected a college solely as a means to seduce my

brother. I mean, Jesus, how did you think this was going to end between us?"

"Don't do this, Sawyer." I say it softly, tears threatening behind my eyelids. I don't beg, and I don't cry, as a general rule. But I'm not sure I can keep that record intact right now.

"It's done."

"You're an asshole."

"I am." Sawyer gives a slight nod. "Your brother tried to warn you, didn't he?"

Wow.

It's true. Eric did try.

I didn't listen.

I flick my eyes to the ceiling, trying to make the tears recede without an obvious swipe to my face.

"I get bored and I move on." Sawyer sighs. "So thanks. Thank you." That comes out a little softer than the words preceding it but he might as well have punched me with the words.

Thank you? For what? Falling in love with him? The mind-blowing sex? Making him laugh? Or leaving his office quietly now that he's dismissed me?

"Fuck you."

Forty-Four

I don't say anything else after that. I turn around and leave his office, grateful Sandra's desk is still empty because the tears are falling down my face.

I walk quickly, my head down so nobody I might pass in the hallway sees my face. My feet make barely a sound on the office carpeting, a soft thump likely only audible to me. I reach the elevator bank and punch the down button, grateful I'm waiting alone, the area blessedly quiet.

An elevator arrives and I get in, hit the lobby button and slump into the corner, allowing the elevator itself to hold me up. A choked sob escapes before I sniffle it in, wiping my face off with the sleeves of my shirt. The elevator slows and I groan as it comes to a stop to allow other passengers to get on. And again two floors later. And the one after that. I cannot catch a break today.

I keep my eyes on the floor but I know everyone can hear me making that sniffle-snort noise you make when you're sucking in tears. I wonder what they think of me, a random girl huddled in the corner of the elevator trying not to cry. Then I remember I might not be so random after all. I may have met some of these people at the party on New Year's Eve. I'm not looking up to check. I'm humiliated enough for one day.

The elevator reaches the lobby and I put one foot in front of the other, the door out of this place my only goal at present. My shoes squeak on this floor.

Someone holds the door for me when I get there, and I say,

"Thank you," as I walk through.

Thank you. I laugh. Thank you is an appropriate response when someone holds the door. It's not an appropriate goodbye during a breakup. What an idiot.

I use the crosswalk to cross the four lanes of traffic that circle Logan Square. It's a circle really. A big circular pie of green space in downtown Philadelphia separated by slices of sidewalk leading to a fountain in the middle. It's empty now, drained for winter. Patches of half-melted ice and small islands of snow dot the fountain's surface.

I sit on the edge then swing my legs over, stepping into the fountain, because why not? How many chances do you get to walk around a dry fountain? I stuff my hands in my pockets and walk to the center, passing a stone frog the size of a small child, its mouth gaping, ready to erupt a stream of water as soon as the weather permits. I reach the fountain a few steps later, walking around it, getting an up-close view of the three statues. There's a girl with a swan on her head. A woman with a swan on her head. And a reclining man reaching for a bow or sword behind his back. There's a large fish on his head. I decide they make as much sense as Sawyer does and take a seat next to sword guy.

Pulling my knees up to my chest, I dig in my bag for my wallet then dump all the change I can find into my hand.

I hope you get diarrhea, Sawyer, is my first wish as I hurl a dime across the empty fountain. *I hope you're plagued with a shoddy internet connection.* That wish gets a quarter. *I hope your next girlfriend snores. I hope you get a flat tire on the turnpike.* Wait, that one is kind of dangerous. Well, fuck him. I lob a penny into the air, watching it hit the cement and roll. *I hope your flight is delayed. Every flight. I hope your cell battery is low and the power goes out. I hope...*

God, I suck at this.

I hope one day you realize what a huge mistake you just made and you never get over me.

I propel the remaining change in my hand across the fountain with the force of a professional pitcher. The coins fly through the air before raining down on the cement. All I hear is the white noise in my ears.

My mind spins but I feel nothing. Empty. I feel empty. I wrap my arms around my bent knees and stare at Sawyer's building until my butt is numb and my nose is running. Then I get up and walk to the opposite side of the fountain where I got in, walking towards 20th Street where I can grab a cab back to school.

Goodbye, Sawyer.

45

"So." Chloe's back from the showers down the hall and running a comb through her hair.

"So," I repeat back, not looking at her. I'm busy.

"So are you going to, I don't know, maybe take a shower today?" she prods.

"Why would I do that?"

"Because you smell, Everly. That's why."

I pull a bottle of room spray out from my desk drawer without looking at her and spray it over my head, the mist landing in my hair and on my hands. I don't care. I keep my eyes on my laptop, my finger scrolling until I find something I like. My full attention is needed on this project.

"Problem solved," I tell her.

"Um, no. No, it's really not." Chloe tidies up her side of the room and stuffs her laptop in her bag, getting ready to head out for the day.

"I'll shower tomorrow. I'm busy."

"You said that yesterday. What are you working on?"

"Pinterest."

"That's helping how?"

"It's very therapeutic."

She walks behind my chair and peers at my laptop. "Sawyer Camden is a dick," she reads out loud, viewing the board of pictures I've created about crappy ex-boyfriends. She nudges my hand out of the way and scrolls through for a minute.

205

"Yeah, no." She snaps the laptop lid closed. "This isn't helping."

"Just go to class, Chloe." I open the laptop again and hit a key to bring it to life.

"It's Saturday."

Oh.

"And I'm not bringing you another can of Pringles."

Oh, no, she didn't.

"So you're gonna have to get up and leave this room."

Fine. I don't need to eat.

"One more thing," she says, pulling open the door with one hand and waving a little canister at me with the other. "The fish haven't eaten yet today. And I'm gonna be gone all day. So they're going to be hungry if you don't get off your ass and leave this room. Bye!" The door swings shut behind her, and I realize the canister of fish food was in her hand.

Whatever. They're goldfish. I don't care.

Except. Except that they're looking at me. I tap my fingertip on the glass and Steve waves his little fin excitedly. He really does. The little guy is totally into me. And then Stella swims to the top looking for food.

Fucking Chloe. I grab my stuff and head to the showers.

Thirty minutes later I'm outside, headed towards the Wawa on Spruce. It's nice out, if you're into that sort of thing. Nice weather, sunshine, love. I'm not, so it doesn't matter. I enter the convenience store, the automatic door swooshing to grant me access, and head for the chip aisle. I grab half a dozen cans of Pringles then head to the coffee counter and place an order for a mocha mint latte. It's so much better than the grasshopper latte we sell at Grind Me. Plus, it doesn't have a stupid bug name. I pop open one of the cans of Pringles while I wait and shove a stack of four into my mouth. I catch a guy judging me for my life choices but I stare back while shoving another stack of chips into my mouth and he looks away.

When my drink is ready I pay for everything and exit the store. There's an independent pet supply store I like on Baltimore Avenue less than a mile from here so I head in that direction, cutting over to Baltimore on University Avenue.

There are a lot of people out today, with the nice weather and all. I loop the Wawa bag full of Pringles over my forearm and sip my latte as I walk. And I guess it doesn't suck to be showered and wearing a fresh hoodie and yoga pants. Then I see a silvery blue Porsche like Sawyer has and the Pringles feel like a shoe lodged in my gut. It's not his car—the license plates are different—but how many stupid little things are going to remind me of him?

I give up on blocking him from my mind and cave in to replaying every moment we've had together over the last eight weeks. The sex tape pisses me off the most. You make a sex tape with someone and they break up with you. Unbelievable. The Sawyer of the last week is nothing like the man I know him to be. I cannot have been that wrong about him. Something isn't right.

I reach the pet shop and push through the wood and glass door, immediately stopping to coo at an adorable kitty chilling in a large window display, set up to provide temporary housing while waiting for an adopter. She's a long-haired calico named Shaggy. She puts her paws on the glass and leans in to inspect me. Not a kitten—she's two, according to the sheet outside her enclosure. So she knows what it's like to be happy and then get dumped. I should totally adopt her. I could sneak her into my dorm room. We'd snuggle every day and I'd let her know that unlike certain men, I won't get sick of her in a couple of months. We'd be together forever. There's even a nice view from my dorm window and a ledge perfect for a cat.

I'm losing it.

Plus, Debbie, the resident advisor on my floor, is a huge bitch and would probably call animal control and get me expelled. I don't know why she hates me so much. So I locked myself out of my room a couple of times very early in the morning. Who hasn't? And the wallpaper I hung in our room is that self-adhesive removable stuff. Sheesh.

I move past the front door and move to the selection of fish food, picking a canister off the shelf as a white paw reaches out from underneath the display to swipe at my shoelace. I crouch down to scratch Molly behind the ears. She's the resident store cat, living there full time. There's nothing better than a store cat, I think as she squeezes out from under the shelving unit for a more serious petting.

"How long has Shaggy been here?" I ask, nodding to the front window as I pay for my fish flakes.

"Oh, a month or so now," the owner tells me. "Such a sweet cat."

"I wish I could take her," I say, looking longingly at the window. "But I live in a dorm room so it's not really an option right now."

"She'll find a home when the time is right," she says, smiling and handing me my change. I toss the fish flakes in the bag with my Pringles and head out, stopping outside to tap my finger against the glass and wish Shaggy luck.

Forty-Six

I retrace my steps down Baltimore back towards my building on campus. By the time I pass 40th Street I'm done being sad about Sawyer. Now I'm pissed. And somewhat curious. But mostly pissed. Something was off last week when I met him at his office, on his birthday. And something happened to make him cancel on me the following weekend. Why didn't he talk to me about it?

Instead he reevaluated me. That's what he said, reevaluated. Like I'm a business acquisition. But Sawyer has never been that guy. He was every bit as in love with me as I am with him. I know it, yet I keep replaying that breakup in my head. His tone of voice, bringing up his brother. Maybe he never loved me. Maybe I was just a challenge. Seducing the girl with a silly childhood crush on his brother.

Stupid. That's stupid. Don't be that girl, I tell myself. Don't let him make you doubt your worth. Don't allow him to make you question what was the most honest, real relationship you've ever had. He doesn't get that back. It was real.

He could have been faking it, toying with me, but he's not that good an actor. *No one* is that good an actor.

Chloe's in the room when I get back. I snort out loud when I see her sitting at her desk, tapping away on her computer.

"Out all day, huh?" I say, tossing the bag of Pringles and fish food on my bed, then shrugging out of my coat.

"I only said all that to get you out of the room. I just ran to the library," she replies. "And I fed the fish." She nods to the

209

canister that's been returned to my desk.

"I walked two miles to buy more fish food!"

"Sorry, you needed an intervention." She doesn't seem very sorry. "Besides, you seem happier. I think the walk did you good."

"I guess."

"So what are you going to do today?" Chloe inquires, standing up and rooting through the Wawa bag. She pulls out a can of barbecue-flavored Pringles and pops them open.

"I think I'm going to stalk Sawyer."

"That sounds about right." She nods. "Glad to see you're back to your old self."

"Do you want to help? It'll be just like old times. Except we'll be spying on Sawyer, not Finn. And we'll be spying at the Ritz-Carlton instead of from the attic vents in my parents' house."

"Hmm." Chloe pretends to think. "Tempting, but I think I'll pass."

"This cannot be it, Chloe." I blow out a breath and sit on the edge of my bed. "How can he just end things like this? I mean, was I imagining things between us that weren't there?"

"No," she says quietly, running her finger around the potato chip can. "I've never seen a man look at a woman the way he looked at you. The guy is crazy about you."

"Was. He was crazy about me."

"He hasn't changed his Facebook relationship status."

"He probably forgot."

"Because Sawyer Camden is a man who forgets the details, Everly?" Chloe shakes her head. "I don't think so."

I gnaw on my lip. I know what she's saying is true. Now what am I going to do about it?

Forty-Seven

I change into something a little more sleuth-worthy and fix my hair and makeup. It's important to look your best when spying. Actually, I have no idea if that is true, but looking your best never hurts. And my nails... I shake my head. I've got chipped ten-day-old Porn-A-Thon still on my fingers. That will not do.

I pull the nail polish box out from under my bed and rifle through it, weighing my options while I remove what's left of the old polish. Ugh. Most of these will not work. I find a bottle named Fake It Till You Make It and unscrew the cap. I bought this for job interviewing this spring, but looking at the shimmery gold polish it's probably better suited for spying than interviewing. Very 007. I think. I've only seen one Bond film, back in high school, and my attention was focused on giving my boyfriend a handjob, to be perfectly honest.

Anyway, it'll do.

I give my nails a quick polish followed by a clear topcoat, then lean back on my bed, waving my hands a bit while I wait for them to dry. I've got to strategize. I have no idea if he's home or not, or even if that matters. What am I intending to do? Use my keys to break into his place? Is it breaking in if I have a key? What if he changed the locks already? I don't think so, though. Just like he didn't change our relationship status on Facebook. I don't think he's changed the locks or deactivated the ID card that gives me access to his building.

But what is my plan? I have no idea if he's home or not. I can't waltz into his apartment if he's home. Why do I even want to waltz into his apartment? What am I going to find there? I could use my ID card and break into his office. But I'm not sure if the door to his office is locked on the weekends. I know I can get access to the building, but can I get access to his office? What difference would it even make? I rifled though his desk the first time I was in his office and didn't find a single interesting thing. And computer hacking is way beyond my skill level.

I could call Sandra. But no. It would make her a nervous wreck to be put in the middle. I can't do that to her. Besides, she's loyal to Sawyer, as she should be.

So I'll have to wing it.

"Wish me luck," I tell Chloe while sliding my shoes on. I'm definitely not wearing the Louboutins today. As much as they would blend in at the Ritz, they're not exactly spy gear. Plus, they make a tapping noise when I walk on a polished surface and you never know when you're gonna need a silent getaway.

"Good luck! I'll keep my cell phone on in case you need me to bail you out of jail later."

"You're a good friend, Chloe," I tell her, freeing my ponytail from under my coat.

"Not really." She shakes her head, smiling. "I'm secretly just happy I'm finally getting a crack at the Pringles," she says, shaking the can. "You don't share when you're sulking."

I cab it over to Sawyer's, then hover outside on the sidewalk, the doorman smiling brightly, hand on the door ready to grant me access. What am I doing? Stupid. This is stupid. The residential lobby isn't large enough to hide in. I can't very well just sit there. And he'd likely take the elevator straight to the parking garage anyway. *Nice plan, Everly.*

I turn around and walk, stuffing my hands in my coat pockets. Dilworth Park is just around the corner in front of City Hall. I need to regroup. I arrive at the park a minute later. It's pretty dead—being the first weekend in February isn't helping, nice weather or not. I walk around the large rectangle of dormant lawn towards the temporary ice rink that workers are taking apart. I wander in that direction and watch for a bit, the walls of the rink coming down and being loaded into a waiting truck, backed up onto the pavement in preparation.

Nearby a couple of kids screech, playing tag as they run along beside their mother, pushing a stroller with another kid.

I head towards the cafe on the north end of the park, but I don't stop. Love Park is just across the street. The place Sawyer and I had our first date, outside at the Christmas Village. The Christmas setup is long gone, of course. But it doesn't stop me from walking the park and remembering every detail of that first date, complete with a blush remembering how it ended.

Signs indicate the park will be closing soon for renovations and I wonder what will become of the famous Love sculpture that the park is unofficially named for during the renovation. I walk in the direction of the sculpture, jockeying for space amongst tourists and locals alike taking selfies with the sign behind them. Sawyer and I took one too. It's the lock screen picture on his phone.

He's mine.

I'm getting him back.

I cross John F Kennedy Boulevard heading back toward the residential tower at the Ritz-Carlton. I'm just gonna knock on his door. I'll go in, I'll take the elevator up and knock on his door. And if he doesn't answer I'm going to let myself in. I'll sit on his couch and wait until he comes home, however long I have to. I will make him tell me what the hell is going on. He'll admit that he's a jerk, we'll have makeup sex and this whole stupid breakup will be over.

Easy.

I walk down 15th Street until I reach the crosswalk at Market Street, then cross over to the Dilworth Park side. I can cut back through the park on my way to the Ritz-Carlton. I'm doing just that when I spot the man himself.

He's standing at the north edge of the large rectangle of

lawn, one foot propped on the curb that separates the lawn from the concrete that covers the rest of Dilworth Park. His hands are in his pockets, elbows bent at an easy angle. He doesn't appear to be watching anything, just standing there. So weird. My steps falter. I'm unprepared to confront him here, outside. So I stop and watch him for a moment, still confused about what he's doing.

He takes one hand out of his pocket and rubs at his forehead, his face tense, like he might have a headache. Oh my God. Maybe he's sick. He was rubbing at his forehead on his birthday too. And in his office, when he broke up with me. He's probably really sick and he didn't want to put me through that. Idiot. I'd walk through anything with him.

Then a petite blonde woman a few years older than me walks towards him. She's in jeans and boots, flat with cute laces. Her hair is pulled back in a low ponytail, and she's zipped up in a light winter jacket. He sees her and his face clears, a wide smile replacing the worry that was there a moment ago.

Fucking hell.

Forty-Eight

My stomach churns, the coffee-and-potato-chip combination doing nothing to help me at the moment. My eyes are glued to the scene, and I momentarily forget that I'm standing in plain sight watching this unfold, not even considering a place to hide. Not that there is one. There's nothing but concrete, open lawn, a half-dismantled ice rink and a couple of entrances to the subway system covering the entire area.

So I stand rooted to the spot I'm in, just staring.

Which allows me to clearly see a small brown-haired boy dash past the blonde and throw himself at Sawyer. And because I'm so lucky, it gives me a direct view of Sawyer catching the boy and swinging him up in his arms, precisely as the traffic lulls, letting me hear the boy as clearly as if I were sitting in a cinema with state-of-the-art surround sound.

"Daddy!"

Don't worry. My luck holds out. Because I get a glimpse of Sawyer's face too. Of the happiness, reverence and devotion spelled out across his features, clear as day.

I'm not confused.

This isn't a joke.

That's his kid.

His walking, talking kid. A person. A child I've never heard a single reference to.

The blonde catches up and leans in, ruffling the kid's hair. The movement causes Sawyer's eyes to turn in my direction, landing on me. It jabs my stomach like a professional blow.

I whirl around, heading back to the crosswalk, but the light is green and cars are whizzing past. I'm trapped on this side of the street, at least for another couple minutes, which is a lifetime too long. I run down the stairs instead, the stairs leading to the subway, enclosed by a fancy glass ski-slope-looking structure from the street. I grab a handrail as I race down the steps. I probably need another twenty steps before I can disappear from view. Focus. One foot in front of the other.

"Everly!"

Oh, he wants to talk now? Yeah, no.

I hit the bottom step and freeze, unsure which way to turn. I've never actually used the Philadelphia subway system before. I quickly figure out the flow of pedestrian traffic though, and fall in line, blindly following the people in front of me. Until we reach a turnstile and I realize I don't have a transportation card or whatever one needs to swipe to make the gate lift and grant me escape. I stop dead, causing the person behind me to knock into me with an, "Oof."

I mutter an apology and move to the side and I have a full three seconds of hope that I've ditched Sawyer before he's there, his hand on my arm.

I throw up on his shoes.

He holds my hair, a perfect gentleman, while I throw up everything that I've eaten today on his stupid shoes.

"Now you've ruined Pringles for me too. I hate you!" I push away from him, wiping my mouth with my sleeve, and walk back to the stairs. I go up a lot slower than I went down. Arms crossed over my chest, chin down. He's right behind me. I know he's there but he's quiet, just following me.

I get back to ground level and look around. The blonde and the little boy are gone.

"Where'd they go?" I circle back to him in a flurry. "They were just here, I saw them."

Wait. Maybe I'm just crazy. Like I'm having a mental break or something. I probably need a head CT.

"I sent them home, back to my place."

No, not crazy. He's a dick.

"Everly, please," he says, bringing my attention to his face. "I'm sorry."

His face, that's the Sawyer I know. Sincere. Honest.

"What in the hell is going on?" I ask him, my eyes darting back and forth across his face.

"Why are you here?"

"Why am I here? Fuck you, Sawyer." I shove a finger in his chest. "Why is that kid calling you Daddy? Who is that woman? You can't be married. Finn wouldn't have been happy for us when we started dating if you already had a wife. My brother would have mentioned it for sure. Unless you've been hiding her in another city. Oh, my God. Do you have a secret family, Sawyer? Or did you already replace me with a new girlfriend? With a kid who calls you Daddy? How long has this been going on?"

"Okay. Slow down, breathe." He nods to the cafe across the park. "Let's sit."

I shake my head.

"I didn't want you to see that. Him. I..." He trails off. "You can't spy on my kid, Everly."

His kid. I swallow the lump in my throat and fight to keep my knees steady.

"Fine. Let's sit."

We walk over to the cafe in silence, Sawyer opening the door for me while I grab a table in the corner and sit. He brings a tray of drinks over a few minutes later, setting it down on the table between us. Bottled water, hot tea, coffee, hot chocolate. I take a swig of water then pull the tea cup between my fingers.

"I wasn't spying on your kid. I didn't even know he existed."

"Neither did I, until last week."

"The same time you turned into a royal dick."

"Yeah," he agrees, a small smile on his face. "About that time."

"What's his name?"

"Jake." A smile spreads across his face when he says it.

"How old is he?"

"Four." He says it softly, as if it pains him.

I take that in. He's missed out on four years with his son.

"Is that his mother?"

"No." Sawyer scoffs. "His nanny."

"So when do I get to meet him?"

"Meet him?" Sawyer's eyebrows are raised, his face questioning. "I broke up with you."

"You didn't mean it." I say it confidently, then falter. "Unless you don't think I'm good enough for him? Is that why you ended things with me so abruptly?"

He pauses, and I die a little bit inside.

"Maybe in a few years," he begins before trailing off.

"I'm sorry. Did you just suggest we get back together in a few years?" I'd be surprised if my eyebrows were still on my face, I've raised them so high in disbelief.

"This isn't what you want. You don't want a child right now. You've said it enough times. And this kid..." He rubs at his forehead in a gesture I'm beginning to recognize as stress. "It's messy, Everly."

"And I don't do messy," I say, filling in the blanks.

"You're young, Everly. You were still a teenager when Jake was born. You deserve to have the life you want, the one you've imagined for yourself."

"The one where I don't have kids for another five to seven years? And I don't have to deal with exes, and custody sharing, and coordinating his kids and our kids for weekends and holidays and summer vacations?"

He nods.

"I don't want a baby right now, Sawyer." I shake my head. "I don't. But Jake isn't a baby, and hell, even if he was, I'd love him. Because he's yours."

"It can't be that simple. You have a vision for your life, and you didn't sign up for this."

"I didn't sign on for you either, remember? I thought I was in love with your brother, but I was wrong. And it didn't stop you, because you were right, Sawyer. You were right about us."

"I love you, but I don't know if it's enough."

"It's enough, and I can edit."

"You can edit?" He's smiling now.

"I can edit the vision I had for my future, for our future. Just as long as you're in it."

"I'm going to have Jake full time. It's not a weekend thing. His mother..." He stops, rubs his forehead. "His mother is in prison. He'll be a teenager before she's out. But I have no idea what the future looks like. She might want back into his life at that point. He might want to see her. It'll be messy, Everly. "

"Is he okay?"

"I don't think he even misses her." Sawyer shakes his head in disbelief. "He barely remembers her as far as I can tell."

"How long has she been—" I pause, not sure how to word it. "Gone?"

"Ten months," he says, drumming his fingers on the table. "He's been living with one of his nannies. Do you really think you want this? Both of us? Because Jake has to be my priority. I have a lot of time to make up for. And..." He blows out a breath. "I don't think he was her priority."

"Give me a chance, Sawyer. Tomorrow we'll have a date. A family date, the three of us."

"Okay," he agrees. He looks doubtful, but he agrees.

Forty-Nine

"I'm going to be a mom!" I announce as I stroll through the door an hour later.

Chloe puts down her pen and turns to me. "So the stalking went well then? You're back together and pregnant now?" She looks at the clock. "All before five o'clock. Well done."

"Not pregnant. Sawyer has a son." I kick off my shoes and pop open a can of Diet Sun Drop before sitting on the edge of my bed, legs crossed.

"Wait, what?" Chloe looks confused. "I thought you were joking."

"Nope," I say, swinging my foot. "Oh! Do you know what this means, Chloe?"

"Um, it means a lot of things," she says, concern marring her forehead.

"I get to be a MILF without going through labor."

"Yeah, no. That wasn't my first thought."

"Anyway, we're going on a date tomorrow. The three of us." I set my soda down and open my laptop, propped up on my knees.

"So Sawyer and you are back together?"

"Yes." I nod. "Not exactly."

"Yes, not exactly?"

"He's a little hesitant. He doesn't think I'm into children." My hands fly over my keyboard as I talk. "But there's one thing Sawyer Camden doesn't know about me."

"What's that?" Chloe asks, getting up to dig into our snack

pile.

"That I, Everly Jensen, am one half of the most popular babysitting duo that Ridgefield, Connecticut ever saw."

Chloe grins. "We were a good team."

"The best," I agree and smile when I find what I'm looking for online, then send Sawyer a text telling him to pick me up tomorrow at 10:45 am.

******

I leave my room at 10:30 the next morning, intending to be outside when Sawyer arrives so he doesn't have to park the car and get out with Jake. But I find him waiting for me in the lobby instead, a miniature version of himself beside him. I'm pretty sure I ovulate at the sight, which I know is scientifically unlikely as I'm on the birth control pill, but I'm glad I'm not going home with Sawyer today all the same.

They're standing in Sawyer's usual spot, near the mail boxes, leaning against the wall with their hands in their pockets in identical poses. Sawyer's wearing jeans and a grey sweater. Jake's in jeans and a navy sweater with a child-sized neck tie over that. It's navy and red striped and makes no sense with his outfit, as he's not wearing a collared shirt.

"Hi." I smile at them both as I approach. "I was going to meet you outside so you didn't have to park."

Jake shakes his head. "When you pick up your friend who is a girl, you park your car and go inside." He looks up at Sawyer for confirmation. "Right, Daddy?"

"Right, buddy." Sawyer nods back, the corners of his eyes creased in amusement. They obviously had a conversation about this when they parked.

"Well, thank you." I bend down to Jake's level. I don't bend over at the waist and loom over him. I hate that. I bend at the knees so our heads are level and extend my hand to him. "I'm Everly."

He shakes my hand very seriously and tells me his name is Jake. Then Sawyer swings him up in his arms and we head outside.

"What's with the tie?" I whisper to Sawyer while we walk to the car.

He shakes his head. "Hell if I know. I was wearing a tie when I met him. He asked for one of his own and wears it every day." We arrive in the parking lot and Sawyer guides me to a Porsche Cayenne and opens the passenger door for me.

"We open car doors! Right, Daddy?" Jake grins at me from Sawyer's arms and I have to bite my lip to keep from laughing. He's so stinking cute.

"Nice SUV." I wink at Sawyer as I hop up into the vehicle. Sawyer buckles Jake into his seat in the back and then we're off, arriving fifteen minutes later at the Please Touch Museum. My research tells me this is the place to visit with a kid on a Sunday afternoon in February.

Sawyer buys our tickets and we drop our coats off in the coat check room then head towards the center past the information desk.

"Which do you like better, cars or rockets?" I ask Jake, consulting the paper map we picked up at the door.

"Cars!"

"Off to roadside attractions it is then," I say and we head left to a series of interactive exhibits where Jake pretends to drive a bus, collect tolls and fill a car with gas. After that we visit the space station exhibit where Jake gets to pretend he's a space shuttle pilot.

But we quickly find out his favorite exhibit is the ShopRite Supermarket on the lower level. He zips down the play grocery store aisles with his child-sized grocery cart with absolute glee, filling it with food till it spills out the top.

"We can take him to Whole Foods next weekend," Sawyer comments. "Totally blow his mind."

I laugh, but I'm secretly glad he said 'we.'

We stop for lunch at the museum cafe. Sawyer and I eat burgers while Jake eats half a hot dog and about a dozen cheese-flavored crackers.

"Is that supposed to freak me out?" Sawyer asks me,

expression serious. "He only eats half of everything. Maybe I should take him to a doctor?"

I place my hand over his and point out that they give out the same-sized hot dog to every kid and a four-year-old isn't likely to finish as much of it as an older kid. He nods and relaxes.

We visit the river adventures exhibit after lunch and Jake gets his tie soaked racing sailboats. He wrings it out and then we visit the carousel.

"I want the cat," he tells me while Sawyer is buying him a ticket.

"I'm not sure there's a cat on the carousel, buddy." We're holding hands watching the animals whiz past from outside a gated area that surrounds it.

"There is. I saw it," he tells me, brow furrowed in concentration as he looks for it again.

The museum employee operating the ride confirms there is indeed a cat. Forty horses, four cats, and a small assortment of other animals. But Jake is firm on the cat, waving to us on each rotation of the carousel.

"This is fun," I say, nudging Sawyer with my elbow.

He smiles in return, that dimple flashing. "It's forever though, Everly. Today is fun, but the reality is he's with me now. All the time. You and I will never have spontaneous weekend trips and sex on the kitchen counter at noon."

"Would you dump me if I got pregnant?"

"No," he says with a long sigh, knowing where I'm going with this.

"It's not any different to me, Sawyer."

"But he's not yours. You can walk away, Everly. I won't blame you for walking away. But if you're going to stay, you've got to stay. He's been through enough already."

"When we first got together and I told you about my perfect dream life you told me life wasn't always that neat."

He nods.

"You also told me we'd get it right," I remind him, pointing a finger between us. "Together. So we're going to get it right,

Sawyer. And we can still have spontaneous weekend trips, you know. We might have them at Disney, but we can have them. I'll give you the kitchen counter sex, that's probably out from now on. But to be honest, your counters are really hard. I can live without kitchen counter sex."

He runs a hand behind his neck and nods.

"He is mine, by the way. Jake is. If he's yours, then he's mine too."

"Okay," he agrees softly, wrapping his arm over my shoulders.

"Where did he come from, Sawyer?" I tilt my head back to look at him, hoping I'm not overstepping my bounds.

"Well, Everly, when two adults take their clothing off, and the male adult sticks a part of his body into the female adult, sometimes—"

"Stop!" I punch him, laughing. "You know what I meant."

"Rebecca used to work for me," he says, stepping back and pinching the bridge of his nose briefly. "We dated. It was..." He pauses, thinking. "It wasn't serious. She was convenient for me, if I'm being brutally honest. And I was an opportunity for her."

"An opportunity how?" I ask, not liking the word.

"She embezzled five million dollars from me and disappeared about a week before Gabe caught onto the missing funds." He shakes his head. "I can only assume she had no idea she was pregnant when she left, because Jake would have been a much bigger payout for her. Hell, I'd have given her everything for him." He grips the divider in front of us, circling the carousel, his knuckles white.

"But instead she disappeared and changed her name. I have no idea what her end game was, if she was going to come back at some point looking to exchange him for the charges against her being dropped. I don't know and she's not cooperating."

"But she's in prison?" I clarify.

He nods, smiling. But it's a sad smile, rueful. "Federal charges. She got caught on identity theft and tax evasion. They haven't even added her sentence for the embezzlement yet.

Embezzlements, I should say. I wasn't the only one."

"I'm sorry," I tell him, and I am. The betrayal is so severe, there's nothing I can say to lessen it.

"The worst part is, I don't think she even wanted him. From what I can piece together, she only ever spent a few weeks at a time with him before leaving again. Looking for her next mark, I suppose."

I nod, even though I can't understand any of that.

"I didn't want him either." He says it softly, and I look up, surprised. "At first, when we realized there was this kid, and the timing was lining up to indicate that he was mine..." He shakes his head. "I wanted that DNA test to be negative more than anything." His lips twist ruefully. "And then I met him, and within a minute I couldn't imagine how I'd lived even a day without him."

The carousel stops and we walk hand in hand to the exit, Jake flying out with a smile on his face.

"He's exactly where he should be, Sawyer."

Fifty

The following weekend we take him to a paint-your-own-pottery place. When I arrive at Sawyer's I find a much older woman has replaced the young blonde nanny I spotted with him the week before. I ask Sawyer about it and he explains that Vanessa was one of several nannies and only agreed to come to Philadelphia for a couple of weeks while Alice made arrangements to move from Washington.

"Thank fuck." I sigh in relief.

Sawyer raises his eyebrow so I elaborate. "Look, I've been more than understanding about your young, attractive assistant. But a beautiful young woman living under the same roof as you? It was testing the limits of my incredibly mature and generous nature."

"You were jealous of Vanessa?" His mouth twitches.

"Um, lemme think," I say, tapping my lip in pretend concentration. "Yes."

"Because you'd like to live with me?"

"Maybe." I mock shrug.

"I'll keep that in mind, Boots," he says, pulling me close. "And I'll let you in on a little secret."

"What's that?"

"I own the unit next door. She was staying there. Also, she's married, hence her need to get back home. And most importantly, she wasn't you. So none of the rest of it matters."

"Smooth, Camden."

He grabs a kiss and sneaks in a feel of my ass.

"Why do you own the unit next store?"

"Why not?" He shrugs. "I bought this place during construction. I didn't want a neighbor so I bought both the units on this floor. I thought I might eventually need the space for a personal security team. I wasn't planning on nanny quarters, but there you have it."

"So Alice is staying there as well?"

"She is," he says, trailing kisses down my jaw. "Are you jealous of a woman old enough to be my mother?"

"No, actually. I was just wondering how much privacy we'd have later and how sound a sleeper Jake is."

"Sleeps like a champ." Sawyer grins.

After we paint pottery—Jake picks a cat and paints it orange, Sawyer and I paint mugs—we return to the condo for Jake's nap. He falls asleep on the drive home and barely stirs while Sawyer carries him through the parking garage, onto the elevator and into his room.

"How much longer will he nap? I don't even care if you say ten minutes. I'll take a quickie," I say, wrapping myself around Sawyer the second he shuts the master bedroom door closed behind us.

"An hour, at least." He lifts me, my legs wrapping around his waist as he carries me to the bed. "Fuck, I've missed you."

I rip off my shirt as he carries me, dropping it to the floor before he lays me out on the bed, his hands immediately unbuttoning and unzipping my jeans. I lift my hips to assist him in sliding the denim down my legs. My panties quickly follow and then he's on me, flipping my ankles over his shoulders as he inhales me, his arms snaking under my thighs and back over, pinning me open. His thumbs zero straight in, pulling my pussy open while his tongue takes a long, slow sweep up my core.

I buck my hips into his face. I'm so wet I can feel a trail of wetness escape a moment before his tongue cleans it up.

"Do you have any idea how many times I've masturbated to the video on my phone? Of us?"

That was the last time we were together. Over three weeks

ago.

"Do you know how many times I've masturbated to the memory of that video?" I return, digging my hands in his hair and moving his face where I want it. "Zero. Zero times. Because I have a roommate and a communal bathroom. I'm gonna need you to focus."

He laughs. I can feel it more than hear it, the vibration driving me that much closer to where I want to be. Then he skips the single finger and gets right to the point with two, thrusting them in with just the hint of roughness that I like, making my back bow and my toes curl. He covers my clit with an open mouth, flicking me with his tongue and pounding me with his fingers until I come.

I loosen my grip on his head and flop back, chest heaving as my pulse slows. Sawyer slides onto the bed next to me, propped up on one elbow, his face relaxed and happy.

"I love you, Boots." He cups my breast, rolling the nipple between finger and thumb, and it takes me half a second to be ready for more. And to realize he's woefully overdressed.

"I love you too, but I hate your clothes. Why are they still on?" I question, and then they're coming off in a flurry of tangled arms and legs until he's naked and flat on his back. I kneel over him, my knees bracketing his hips as I fist his cock and guide it inside of me, sinking onto him.

We groan together as the length of him slides in to the hilt, the stretch a slight and welcome burn. Then his hands are on my hips, mine overlapping his as he thrusts from below while I control the pace from above, sliding up and down his cock, my tits bouncing with increasing velocity.

I let go of his hands so I can lean forward a bit, bracing my hands on his chest, changing the angle so my clit rubs against him when I rock forward.

We come moments later, my orgasm an instant before his. My pussy pulsing around him sends him over the edge as he grunts his load into me.

I relax onto his chest for a moment before moving myself off of him, and when he slides out of me I immediately notice how much wetter it is without a condom.

"Why did I ever say I didn't want messy?" I joke. I reach a hand down to touch myself—to touch him on myself, really. "This is so fucking hot."

"You know that's going to be leaking out of you for the rest of the day, right?" he asks, placing his hand over mine, rubbing the fluid onto the outside of my pussy.

"This just gets better and better," I murmur.

His dick looks like it'd like to make another run, but Sawyer glances at the clock on the wall and gets up, walking into the bathroom and returning with a wet washrag.

I blush when he uses it to clean me up.

"Everything we do and this embarrasses you?"

"Just a little bit," I respond as something crashes nearby.

We're off the bed and dressed in under a minute, Sawyer out the door seconds before I am.

"It's okay, Daddy," Jake says as I come upon the crime scene. Half a container of apple juice seeps across the kitchen floor. Jake runs a soggy dishtowel through it. "I clean it up. When we make a mess, we clean it, right, Daddy?"

Oh, God. I squeak and cough into my hand while Sawyer gives me a once-over while trying not to laugh.

"That's right, buddy."

"Were you guys having a nap too?" Jake looks up from the floor, eyelashes blinking, and I wonder how many years we have left of his complete unsullied innocence.

Probably not many, but I'm going to enjoy every one of them.

And all the years that follow.

51

A couple weeks later we do take him to a grocery store, but we skip Whole Foods in favor of the Di Bruno's on Chestnut. It's less than a half mile walk from Sawyer's, which means Jake walks about half of it and gets piggyback rides the remainder of the journey. He's thrilled to push a mini-cart around the store while we put real groceries inside of it and it makes his whole day when Sawyer lets him swipe the credit card at checkout.

"We forgot the cookies!" Jake stalls, hand in mine just outside the store.

"We bought everything we need for the cookies, I promise."

A frown mars his brow, the expression so similar to Sawyer's it's hard not to laugh. "We did not get cookies," he tells me, shaking his head back and forth.

"Oh, no, we didn't buy cookies, Jake. We're going to make them. It'll be fun."

He looks at the bag that Sawyer is carrying doubtfully but allows me to piggyback him home.

After naps for everyone, Jake stands on a chair at the kitchen island and helps me. I measure the ingredients and he pours them in the bowl, concern covering his face with each ingredient.

"This goes in cookies?" he asks, dumping the flour. The

eggs get me a worried look and a little sigh. "Are you sure?" He proceeds with the vanilla.

When the first tray of chocolate-chip cookies comes out of the oven his eyes light up and he yells to Sawyer, sitting on the couch, totally within normal speaking range. "We made cookies, Daddy!"

Sawyer strolls over and ruffles his hair, then snags a cookie. "Good job, bud."

"Magic cookies, Daddy," he says, eyes wide. "We didn't cut them."

Sawyer and I exchange a look over his head, equally confused, until I finally get it.

"He means the tubes of cookie dough you buy at the store," I fill in as Jake takes off again, coming back with a piece of construction paper that he carefully folds in half before asking for a pencil. I hand him one as I clean up the cookie mess and pop another tray in the oven while Sawyer eyes my ass and answers Jake's spelling questions.

A few minutes later Jake puts down his pencil and slides the paper over to me. I pick it up. He's made me a card.

Thanks Everly
for the cookies!!!
next can I have
Mr. pants please!!!

I think the drawing on the front is a bookshelf. I open the card and find the following inside.

no!? yes!!!!!

I determine that he wants another Mr. Pants book. We read them together all the time. It's a chapter book series about cats and he's obsessed with them.

I pick up the pencil and circle yes before sliding the card back over. "Of course we can, Jake. Maybe we can go to the bookstore before dinner."

"He has the entire series," Sawyer says, leaning over and looking at the card. "The next book isn't out until June. I keep explaining to him that we have all of them already."

Shit. I just promised something I can't deliver.

"Oh, Mr. Pants!" I exclaim, stalling while I think of a solution. "I thought you meant a real cat. My bad!"

The second the words are out of my mouth I realize what I've just said. So does Jake because he lights up like I've just promised him his own cat. Double shit.

"I'm getting a cat?" His eyes are wide and he drops the card on the counter. "I'm getting a kitty!" And with that he drops the card and takes off down the hall to his bedroom yelling about finding his shoes. He's back a moment later with his tie in one hand, shoes in the other. "Ready!"

Sawyer just looks at me, shaking his head.

"Well..." I drum my fingers on the granite. "You didn't really think me as a parent was going to be all smooth sailing, did you?"

An hour later we're the proud parents of Shaggy, a two-year-old long-haired calico cat. She was still there, in that pet shop on Baltimore, waiting for us. I didn't expect her to be there weeks later. I thought we'd pop in and see who they had available, but there she was, looking like she'd been waiting her whole life for Jake to show up. Jake's lip quivered when he was able to pet her for the first time.

"I can keep her for reals?" he'd asked, tears running down his face.

When we get back to the condo, I let her out of the carrier and explain to Jake that Shaggy's been through a lot, so it might take her a bit to understand that this is her forever home now. Jake nods and tells me that he's going to call her Mr. Pants.

I agree that obviously, that's what we'll call her. Then he runs off dragging a feather toy so Shaggy, Mr. Pants, follows.

"So today went well, I think," I say, glancing away from Sawyer guiltily.

"Hmm," he replies, circling the kitchen island towards me,

a predatory look on his face.

I squeak and try to outrun him but he's on me in a second, tickling me while I try and wiggle away, crying mercy.

Jake thinks this is hysterical and joins in, giggling so hard I'm afraid he might pee.

Sawyer lets me free as Jake asks how long I can stay.

"I can stay till your bedtime, bud." Hopefully a couple hours past, but he doesn't need to know that.

"No," he says, shaking his head. "Are you staying forever too? Like Mr. Pants? Or will you leave sometimes, like a nanny? They leave and take care of other kids. My mom leaves too. I don't know why."

"We're forever friends, Jake." I want to tell him more, explain how much I love him and that I'd never leave him behind, not for anything or anyone. But I settle on that explanation for now and the frown leaves his forehead and a smile lights up his face, so I think I got it right.

Fifty-Two

"I'm gonna write a book," I announce to Chloe when I get back to the dorm that night.

"Okay, sounds good," Chloe says with a yawn as she snaps her laptop shut. "A political thriller? Dorm room cuisine? Wait, I've got it." She snaps her fingers and points at me. "A guide to Christian courtships?"

"A children's book," I advise as I open a blank notebook and a pencil. "About me and Jake."

"Huh," she says, climbing into her bed. "For once, that's not the worst idea you've ever had."

"I know. It's like my entire life has been leading to this moment, don't you think?" I tap the pencil on my notepad and look up.

"That might be just slightly dramatic." She holds up a finger and thumb an inch apart to demonstrate. "But classic Everly."

I work on the book every spare second for a month. Graduation is looming, final exams and papers coming up in every class. Sawyer offers to give me whatever cash I need so I can quit my part-time job at Grind Me, but I tell him no, thank you very much, big daddy. I do ask him if I should get an apartment with Chloe after graduation or not. He says not, but stops short of asking me to move in with him and Jake. Instead he reminds me that he owns the condo next door and the nanny is only using one bedroom, winking as he says it. Time will tell but I think we all know how that's going to end.

I find a place that will turn your work into a book. So I digitalize everything and hand off *Forever Home* to be printed. Just one copy. I drew the pictures myself. It's not the best artwork in the world, but art is subjective, right? It doesn't matter to me, because the only person it was meant for loves it. We read it together every time we're together. It's our story, Jake's and mine. But at its heart it's a story about loving the family you put together, piece by piece. That includes nannies and teachers, friends and grandparents. Cats and dogs too. Even goldfish.

A couple of weeks before graduation Sawyer tells me he wants me to attend a work function with him. Something boring about an acquisition and spouses in attendance. I don't focus on the details other than the when and the what to wear.

He picks me up at school and drives me back to the Ritz-Carlton. I make a production of asking him if he's made up this business dinner in order to lure me to a fancy hotel room for sex, nostalgic about my outburst on our first date.

Now, like then, he tells me we're just parking the car.

Oh, well. A girl can hope.

He takes my hand and we head towards 15th Street, walking through Dilworth Park towards John F Kennedy Boulevard. Love Park is ahead of us, walled off in construction fencing, the year-long park renovation well under way. So I'm surprised when we stop, a security guard opening a gate for us to pass through with a nod from Sawyer.

"What are we doing, Sawyer? The park is closed."

"Just cutting through," he says.

But he leads us further into the park, stopping at a small candlelit table, champagne chilling in an ice bucket beside it.

"I lied," he says.

I like where this is going.

He pulls out a chair and seats me at the table, then sits across from me, face serious.

"Everly, I have something important to talk to you about."

Yes. Yes, you do. Can I squeeze another yes in here? All the yeses.

"What's that?" I ask calmly. I've been wearing Show Me the Ring on my nails for a month.

"Do you think you could delete the *Sawyer Camden is a dick* board from your Pinterest?"

My eyes widen. I so forgot all about that. I make a mental note to never again forget what a little stalker he is.

"Consider it done." I smile. It's loud downtown. Why have I never noticed that before? I hope I don't miss anything important. I focus on Sawyer but he's not saying anything. Just staring at me expectantly.

"Um, now? Did you want me to delete it right this second?"

He raises his eyebrows and nods.

I fumble for the clutch in my lap, my hands a little shaky. I get it out and open up the Pinterest app, pulling up my boards. But it's gone. Replaced by a board named *Marry Me, Everly*. There are hundreds of pictures of the words 'Marry Me.' On coffee cups and neon signs. Spelled out in the sand and written on chalkboards. I'll look at them all later, but right now, Sawyer is on one knee in front of me, a ring in his hand.

"Everly Jensen, will you marry me?"

I must say yes because a moment later the ring is on my finger. It's perfect. A cushion-cut stone surrounded by a perimeter of smaller diamonds that continue around the band.

Of all the rings I've looked at on Pinterest it's the one I loved the most.

Sawyer is filling my glass with champagne when I notice a bottle of nail polish on the table. I recall that it was in his hand, the ring resting around the cap.

"You bought me nail polish?" I question, picking it up. It's orange, my favorite color. I immediately flip it over to see what it's called.

Everly Ever After is printed on the label.

I've never even told him about the nail polishes.

I've said it before—life really has a way of working out for me. My advice? A positive attitude and the ability to be flexible is essential. And a dash of delusion never hurts.

Epilogue

I fell in love with her the moment she walked into the room at my parents' house that Sunday afternoon in November. Love at first sight was a ridiculous notion until Everly.

That first sixty seconds was a punch to the gut. I thought I'd found her and lost her all in the blink of an eye.

As she trailed into the room behind Eric, my brain couldn't process fast enough. Captivated. Before she even said a word. But who was she? Eric had gotten married recently. Was that his new wife? I'd sent a silent fuck you to the universe.

But wait.

Eric wasn't even looking at her. No way that woman was your wife and you weren't looking at her every time she was in the room. And there was something similar about them—the shape of their eyes, the color of their hair. Please God, let that be his sister.

I glanced at Finn, gauging his reaction to our guests, and caught the tiniest flicker of exasperation cross his face. It was brief. So brief I'd think I'd imagined it if not for knowing Finn his entire life. Another piece to this sixty-second puzzle.

Eric called out a greeting and I rose, clapping him on the back and congratulating him on his wedding, but he didn't turn to the woman trailing him at the mention of his marriage. Definitely not his wife. And neither Eric or Finn had bothered to introduce us, likely assuming we'd met somewhere along the way. And that's when it all fell into place for me. I knew exactly who the little bombshell was.

"You're Eric's little sister," I said, and I grinned from ear to ear as she begrudgingly stepped forward to shake my hand and introduce herself.

"Yes, I'm Everly," she said. And I was done.

She was like no woman I'd ever met. High-spirited, to say the least. The most beautiful woman I've ever laid eyes on, certainly. But more than that, she was real. Maybe it was her belief that she was meant to be with my brother that allowed her to drop all pretenses with me. Shooting me dirty looks in my parents' living room, rejecting me all the way back to Philadelphia. I've never been so enraptured. I knew she was attracted to me, yet fighting it tooth and nail, under some insane belief that my brother would be the perfect match for her.

Wooing her became my sole focus. Then keeping her my only concern.

Until Jake came along, knocking my feet right out from underneath me. I had a son. A four-year-old son. And the love of my life was a vivacious twenty-two-year-old who had made it clear that she wasn't interested in having children anytime soon. And worse, I knew her feelings on exes and custody arrangements. Half-siblings and holidays spent divided. I'd never have stood a chance with her if Jake had been in the picture when we'd met.

So what was I supposed to do?

I knew she'd stay if I told her about him. But was that best for her? For Jake? Would I be forcing a child, an instant family, on her that she'd resent later?

So I sent her away.

It fucking killed me. But I sent her away. I assumed she'd find out about Jake eventually, realize that was the reason why. But I thought it'd be months down the line. She'd move on. Find someone new. Someone uncomplicated. And she'd realize it was the right thing, my ending it with her. She could have the life she envisioned for herself without feeling guilty for walking away from me.

But then she showed up that afternoon in Dilworth Park,

and I watched a hundred emotions cross her face when she saw Jake, heard him call me Daddy. I couldn't let her disappear into the subway thinking everything between us had been a lie. And then she surprised me, asking for a chance to meet Jake, to prove that not only could we make it work for us, she wanted to make it work for my son too.

I watched her fall in love with Jake over the next several weeks and it was the most absolute love I've ever witnessed.

Then she wrote him his own book, *Forever Home.* Jake's obsessed with it. And so is the agent I sent it to. He's got an offer for it, an offer and a request from the publisher for an additional two books. I received the email late this afternoon. Now I just need to tell Everly about it. She doesn't think it's good enough for the world to see, but she's been wrong before.

"What are you doing?" I approach her from behind, bending in to nip at her neck and take a peek at what she's up to. I've found it's best to stay up to date with Everly at all times. She's not a girl you want a step ahead of you.

She's curled up in a corner of my couch, all of that remarkable hair piled onto the top of her head in a messy knot. She's wearing something she refers to as yoga pants and an oversized cotton top that's slipping off one shoulder as she taps a key on the laptop. She's beautiful like this. Stunning, really. I can't believe I get to spend the rest of my life with her.

"Research," she tells me, and I think I see a castle on the screen. Not a romantic European castle I can rent in order to fuck her in every room, but a Disney castle.

"For?" I prod.

"The honeymoon."

"Aren't I supposed to plan the honeymoon?" I ask, walking around the couch to sit next to her. I'm not entirely sure how all this wedding planning works, but I seem to recall that traditionally the honeymoon is the groom's job. Then again, Everly isn't exactly traditional.

"Do you want to help?" she asks, brightening. "I was thinking Disneyland Paris," she says. "It's just outside of the city, and I'd love to see Paris with you." She says it hopefully, giving a little tug on her bottom lip with her teeth. "We'd need three suites at the Disneyland Hotel though and it's a bit expensive." She taps her orange-painted nails on the laptop. "But you did say you have almost a billion dollars. So it's probably okay?"

She looks up from the screen to wait for my response and there's not an ounce of mischief there. She's completely serious.

"Sure, it's fine. Whatever you want," I agree. "But why do we need three suites?"

"For our parents and Jake."

Wait, what?

"You want to bring Jake on our honeymoon?" I ask, understanding now why we're headed to Disneyland.

"Well, of course. It's not just about us. Our marriage will be a celebration of us becoming a family. It's a familymoon."

God. My heart explodes when she says that.

"So I was thinking we should bring all of our parents along. Because they have a lot of catching up to do with Jake too. This would give them all a chance to bond."

I was looking forward to a different sort of bonding. But Everly's being beyond gracious to include Jake in our honeymoon. Familymoon. I should focus on that.

"Then if Jake is comfortable with it, he can alternate nights in his grandparents' suites."

I like where this is going.

"And then I thought maybe we could take off for a few nights on our own into the city," she says, clicking on a tab that opens a page to the Paris Four Seasons.

I'm downright delighted that Jake just went down for the night.

And that he still sleeps like the dead.

And that Everly is snapping the laptop closed and taking off her shirt.

I'm a lucky, lucky man.

Acknowledgements

Thank you, from the bottom of my heart for taking the time to read my book. I know your time is precious and I appreciate that you spent some of it with Sawyer & Everly.

Beverly & Kristi, thank you for talking me off the ledge on a regular basis. Your encouragement and feedback at each step in this process are priceless, I'm so lucky to have you as friends and I hope I tell you that enough.

JA Huss, thank you for making my cover & helping with graphics. Just wait till I learn photo shop you'll be so sad!

RJ Locksley, please never stop editing. I can't imagine doing this without you. Please never make me!

Michelle New, thank you for crying when you read the breakup scene. Not gonna lie, it makes me a little proud.

CCL's,
#becausecats

Notes

These notes are filled with spoilers about the book, so if for some reason you've skipped here to read them, don't!

Everly. Holy shit she was so much fun to write. Do you want a little backstory? Originally, I thought Everly ended up with Finn. Actually, let's go even farther back. I think Everly's original name was Jessa. I wanted a J name to go with Jensen, Jessa Jensen. But, as I wrote I was afraid that Jessa was a little too close to Jana, and that was weird. So it had to go.

When I wrote WRONG, I worked in a ton of names of people I knew. Probably 30 names. And one of the people I wanted to include was my great friend Beverly Tubb. Bev was originally a nurse in the exam room during Sophie's appointment at the student clinic. And as some of you caught, when I changed it, I made a huge ass typo. So the nurse in that room is called both Bev and Marie. Oops.

Anyway, I had this epiphany at some point while writing WRONG that I'd drop the B from Beverly & I'd name this girl Everly. And I knew even then that Everly's full name was Beverly Cleary Jensen, because her parents named her after Beverly Cleary. And she'd have a brother named Eric Carle Jensen, named after Eric Carle. So that random bit of information I knew about Everly a long long time ago. Those names were very purposeful, because I adored reading Beverly Cleary and Eric Carle as a child.

So that's how Everly came about. Initially, I was only focused on Sophie & Luke. I wasn't setting WRONG up to have a best friend that I could write about later. But Everly was just so much fun. So I started to think, well maybe. Maybe IF I wrote another book, someday, it could be about Everly. But by then I was pretty far into WRONG. And Everly had already made it clear she believed Professor Finn Camden was the one for her.

So Everly was chasing Finn in the background as I wrote Sophie & Luke's story and I began to worry. How was I going to write Everly's story? I don't read books where the girl chases the guy. I don't like it. I like alpha males that walk in & look at the girl & say MINE. That's what I like to read. So did I want to write a book about Everly chasing Finn? Not really. And then, poof, I knew Finn had a brother. And I knew the brother was THE ONE. The brother would take one look at Everly & think, she's mine. I realized that Everly would end up with Sawyer at that moment in WRONG when Sophie & Everly are in the coffee shop after Thanksgiving. Sophie asks Everly about her weekend and if she made any headway with Professor Camden and for the first time, Everly falters, unsure what is going on. Because I knew that's where the books would cross & in RIGHT she's just met Sawyer & he's driven her home from Connecticut. And she is very very confused. But truthfully, prior to that moment in WRONG I did think Everly ended up with Finn.

Finn & Sawyer's names were coincidence. I do not have any specific love of Mark Twain. Finn was always Finn. And when I decided he had a brother I ended up at Sawyer for several reasons. I thought their parents also had a thing for naming their kids after literary figures and it would be something that Everly & Sawyer could laugh about. But I also recalled somewhere in my memory that Mark Twain was a pseudonym. And as I ran to Wikipedia to check on that I thought, I'll name Sawyer's company after Mark Twain's real name so Everly can connect the dots once she visits his office. Because that scene where Everly shows up in his office all, "I need to see Sawyer Camden," without realizing he owned the place, was firmly in my mind very early on, way back in the middle of writing WRONG. And that scene stemmed from me listening to The Vamps, *Somebody to You* on repeat for months & months. Okay a year. Fine it's still on my favorites playlist. I could clearly envision Sawyer standing in his office as Everly looked around & asked if he was somebody important & Sawyer responding that all he wanted to be was somebody to her.

Mr. Pants - I don't have any tie to the series or author. I read *Mr. Pants Slacks, Camera Action!* months AFTER knowing Mr. Pants would be significant to Jake. The story behind this is, I have a friend that is a librarian at a public school in Hawaii. She runs the occasional fundraiser for books or supplies and I donated to one of them. Shortly after I got the most amazing stack of thank you notes. The best kind, made from construction paper. One of them stood out. I copied it almost word for word into RIGHT. The thank you I received said, *"Thanks Auntie Jana for thos books!!!"* ☺ *next can I have mr. pans pleas!!!* Inside the card was, *"no!? yes!!!!!"*

Attached to the card was a post it from my friend saying, *"Mr. Pants – a series about cats. This kid kills me."*

So I did what any normal person would do. I messaged Debby immediately and asked where the fundraiser for the Mr. Pants books was. Because this kid *needed* Mr. Pants! What did I need to do to get Mr. Pants to this kid? Why was she not giving Mr. Pants to him? Well, it turns out that there were no more Mr. Pants. The library already had all the Mr. Pants books and the next one wouldn't be out for months. Librarian Debby has explained this to the Kindergarteners many times, but still, this little guy walks in and asks for more Mr. Pants on a regular basis. That had to go in the book, clearly.

The nail polishes, they're all real, by the way. I know I could have made up any nail polish name I wanted, but it was weirdly important to me that they actually existed. I'll list them here, if you're so inclined to look for them.

Chapter 11 - Mod About You - OPI
Chapter 12 - Sole Mate purple - Essie
Chapter 21 - A Good Man-darin is Hard to Find - OPI
Chapter 25 - Size Matters - Essie
Chapter 35 - Romantically Involved - OPI
Chapter 39 - Porn-A-Thon - Smith & Cult
Chapter 47 - Fake It Till You Make It - Deborah Lippman
Chapter 52 - Show Me the Ring - Essie
Chapter 52 - Everly Ever After – This one I did make up. ;)

Well, now I've written two books. I just made a face at myself typing that. So weird. I wrote two books! Anyway, I hope I didn't let you down with RIGHT. I still can't believe anyone read WRONG. The last six months are a blur. I thought I'd publish WRONG and a few people would read it. And then, a couple weeks after hitting publish WRONG made the New York Times bestseller list. Hitting that list wasn't even a fantasy in my delusional head. I'm still in shock. And now, as I write this a couple of weeks before RIGHT publishes I am freaking out. Will you like it as much? How will I feel if you don't? Is there a therapist in my area that specializes in book releases? (There's not, I've Googled.)

Until next time, you can catch up with me here:
on Facebook: Author Jana Aston
on Twitter: @janaaston,
on my website: Janaaston.com
or you can catch up with my cat on Instagram: SteveCatnip

Thank you,
Jana

About Jana

Jana Aston is the New York Times bestselling author of WRONG.

After writing her debut novel, she quit her super boring day job to whip up her second novel, RIGHT. She's hoping that was not a stupid idea.

In her defense, it was a really boring job.

CPSIA information can be obtained
at www.ICGtesting.com
Printed in the USA
LVOW11s1321231116

514261LV00003B/146/P